She wasn't sure which of them moved first, but then he was kissing her again.

This was when she should be sensible and stop this, she knew. When she should tell him they needed to go back to being just friends and colleagues. But the way he made her feel...

She opened her mouth and let him deepen the kiss, and the flickers turned into flames.

When he broke the kiss, his pupils were huge, his mouth was slightly swollen and reddened, and there was a slash of color across his cheekbones. She'd guess she was in the same state.

"Well," he said softly. "That wasn't supposed to happen."

"We should be sensible," she said.

He cupped her cheek, his fingers warm and gentle against her skin. "Something about you makes me forget to be sensible, Jess."

"Me, too," she whispered, and leaned forward to kiss him.

Dear Reader,

I'm very much a dog person, and I really wanted to write a book about a dog trainer. Especially after I saw a talent show that was won by a dancing dog—it gave me a lightbulb for a scene. And when my editor suggested that my hero could have a change of career and be a film star...well, that was when my imagination went into overdrive! (And it was also a very good excuse to chat with my friend Daisy Cummins, who happens to be a film director as well as a fantastic author herself, and who was utterly wonderful about letting me grill her—thank you, Daisy.)

I had to be careful not to let the dog take over. Which was very, very difficult, because Baloo has a lot in common with my spaniel. (Except when I wanted to do a bit of research, i.e., teach him how to dance. Byron just lay on his back and put his paws in the air and refused to move. In fact, his main contribution to my research was snoring and stealing shoes, though unlike Baloo he doesn't chew them.)

Luke's wary after being divorced in the public eye. And Jess has a deeply tragic past that makes it very hard for her to move on. Baloo is on her last chance—but she brings Luke and Jess together and gives them the second chance they both need.

The best bit? The proposal scene. I loved, loved, *loved* writing that, and I hope you enjoy it as much as I did!

I'm always delighted to hear from readers, so do come and visit me at www.katehardy.com.

With love,

Kate Hardy

Behind the Film Star's Smile

Kate Hardy

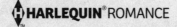

Recycling programs for this product may not exist in your area.

ISBN-13: 978-0-373-74284-4

BEHIND THE FILM STAR'S SMILE

First North American Publication 2014

Copyright © 2014 by Pamela Brooks

This edition published by arrangement with Harlequin Books S.A.

For questions and comments about the quality of this book, please contact us at CustomerService@Harlequin.com.

® and TM are trademarks of Harlequin Enterprises Limited or its corporate affiliates. Trademarks indicated with ® are registered in the United States Patent and Trademark Office, the Canadian Trade Marks Office and in other countries.

Printed in U.S.A.

www.Harlequin.com

R

Kate Hardy lives in Norwich, in the east of England, with her husband, two young children, one bouncy spaniel and too many books to count! When she's not busy writing romance or researching local history she helps out at her children's schools. She also loves cooking— spot the recipes sneaked into her books! (They're also on her website, along with extracts and stories behind the books.) Writing for Harlequin Romance has been a dream come true for Kate—something she wanted to do ever since she was twelve. She's also been writing Harlequin Medical Romance books for years now. She says it's the best of both worlds, because she gets to learn lots of new things when she's researching the background to a book: add a touch of passion, drama and danger, a new gorgeous hero every time, and it's the perfect job!

Kate's always delighted to hear from readers, so do drop in to her website at www.katehardy.com.

Recent books by Kate Hardy

BOUND BY A BABY
A DATE WITH THE ICE PRINCESS
THE BROODING DOC'S REDEMPTION
BALLROOM TO BRIDE AND GROOM
ONCE A PLAYBOY
THE HIDDEN HEART OF RICO ROSSI
DR CINDERELLA'S MIDNIGHT FLING
THE EX WHO HIRED HER

This and other books by Kate Hardy are also available in ebook format from www.Harlequin.com.

For Daisy Cummins, with love and thanks for letting me grill her about film-making!

CHAPTER ONE

OMG. LUKE *MCKENZIE*.

When Jess had taken the assignment from the temp agency to work as a production assistant for a film company, she'd expected it to be a low-budget affair with actors she'd never heard of. Not Luke McKenzie, who'd been named as the most beautiful man in the world for three years running. Luke McKenzie, the favourite actor of both her sister and her best friend, and whose films they dragged her to see at the cinema, even though Jess would rather watch a decent sci-fi movie than sit through a rom-com for the umpteenth time.

Luke McKenzie, who right now didn't look very happy.

Neither did the chocolate Labrador who was sitting beside him, radiating guilt.

Well, this was none of her business. She was meant to be sorting out some paperwork, not gawking at an A-list movie star or listening in to her boss's conversation.

'Jess, can you come here a second, please?' Ayesha Milan, the production manager, called.

'Sure,' Jess said, expecting to be sent on an errand.

'Can you look after Mr McKenzie's dog today?'

Jess froze.

Look after a dog.

That was precisely why she'd left the career she loved and had become a temp. So she'd never have to look after another dog again.

'I...'

'She doesn't bite,' Luke said, rolling his eyes. 'Just steals things and chews them. She seems to have a particular taste for Louboutins.'

Expensive designer shoes. Well, that would explain why he didn't look too happy—the owner of said shoes had probably had a mammoth hissy fit on him when she'd discovered the damage, and replacing them would be far from cheap.

'Jess, are you scared of dogs?' Ayesha asked.

'No-o,' Jess said hesitantly. She wasn't scared of dogs. She was scared of bonding with them. Of having her heart shredded again. It had taken her more than a year to get to where she was now. The thought of having to look after a dog was bringing everything right back to her.

'Then can you take charge of...?' Ayesha looked at Luke to prompt him for the dog's name.

'Baloo.'

'Baloo,' Ayesha finished, looking straight at Jess.

Oh, help.

As a production assistant, Jess was basically meant to do anything she was asked to do. Saying no would be tantamount to cancelling her contract. Even though she'd worked for the temp agency for nearly a year now, it would still make her look unreliable if she walked out of this job less than an hour after she'd started it, leaving the client in a mess. Which meant they'd be less likely to give her any more assignments, and she couldn't afford to lose her job.

But saying yes meant putting herself back in a vulnerable position. Something she really didn't want to do.

'I've got to get back to the set. I don't have time for this. Here,' Luke said, and handed her the dog's lead.

Before Jess could process what was happening, he'd stomped off.

Leaving her with the dog.

'I—look, don't I have other stuff to do for you?' she asked Ayesha, inwardly panicking. Please let her not have to do this. Please.

Ayesha spread her hands. 'The big thing is to keep the stars happy. We have to tiptoe round them.' She sighed. 'I expected Mimi to be the difficult one, not him.'

'Why did he bring the dog on set? Especially if he knows that she chews things?'

Ayesha shrugged. 'I have no idea.'

'He could've brought a crate with him. Where the dog would've felt safe instead of worried by all the people round her, and—' Jess stopped, aware that Ayesha was looking curious.

'You sound as if you know about dogs.'

A degree in animal behaviour and working as a police dog trainer for most of her career had taught Jess a lot. 'A bit,' Jess mumbled.

'Then you'll be the perfect person to look after Baloo,' Ayesha said brightly.

No, she wasn't. She was the last person to look after the dog. Why hadn't she lied and said that she was scared of dogs, or allergic to them? And she was furious at the way the actor had behaved. This was as bad as the socialites who carried a little dog around with them as an accessory. 'If you haven't got time to look after a dog properly, you shouldn't have one,' Jess said. 'I don't care if he's the star of the film. This isn't how you treat dogs.' She frowned. 'My sister and my best friend think he's wonderful. I didn't think he'd be like—well, like *that*, in real life.' Grouchy. Demanding. Whatever the male equivalent of a diva was.

'He never used to be,' Ayesha said. 'I worked on a film with him a couple of years ago, and he was a total sweetheart—he remembered everyone's name, thanked anyone who ran an errand for him, and I think every female member of the crew and cast fell in love with him. Including me, and I'm used to actors being charming. With him, it wasn't acting. He meant it.' She shrugged. 'But he's had a pretty hard time the last year. I think it's changed him.'

Jess remembered seeing the stories about the break-up of Luke McKenzie's marriage in the press. A divorce must be hard enough to deal with, but having the press zooming in on every detail must make it so much worse. And even Carly and Shannon—her sister and her best friend—had admitted that Luke's last film hadn't been quite as good as the previous ones. Not surprising, really: when your life imploded, it was pretty hard to concentrate on your job and do your best. Which was why Jess was focusing on doing something completely different from her old life. 'Even so, you don't just dump your dog on the nearest stranger.'

The dog licked her hand, as if glad that someone was batting her corner, and Jess felt something crack in the region of her heart.

No.

She couldn't do this. She couldn't make herself that vulnerable and open again.

'Wouldn't it be better if she went to the animal handling department?' Jess asked, hoping she didn't sound quite as desperate as she felt.

'They work part-time and they're only on set when we actually need them.' Ayesha looked at her schedule. 'Which isn't today.'

So she had no choice?

'Jess, if you could look after the dog, I'd be really grateful,' Ayesha said. 'I need to keep everything running as smoothly as possible. And if we say we can't do it and give the dog back to him, it's going to affect rehearsals. We start filming this week, so we can't afford any setbacks. The dog chewed Mimi's shoes. I've already had a message from the director to get another pair delivered here by lunch-time. I get the impression that if we refuse to look after her and the dog goes back with Luke, then Mimi's going to walk off set. And it'll take an awful lot to unruffle her feathers and persuade her to come back.'

'Artistic temperament?' Jess asked.

'Let's just say she lives up to her name.'

Mimi—me, me, me, me. Jess got it instantly.

Ayesha blew out a breath. 'Though I'd appreciate it if you didn't repeat any of that.'

Jess remembered what the production manager had told her right from the start: set rules were non-negotiable. What happened on set, stayed on set. No photographs, no social media, no mobile phones, no leaks. Everything within the bounds of the set was to remain a completely separate world. 'Of course not.'

'And if you can get those call sheets for tomorrow sorted while you're looking after the dog, that'd be good.' Ayesha smiled at her.

Dismissed, but nicely so. It looked as if she didn't have a choice in the matter, then. 'OK,' Jess said, and took the dog over to her own desk.

Luke McKenzie hadn't bothered to bring a water bowl with him, or give any information about the dog's feeding schedule. And she had no idea when the movie star planned to come and collect the dog. He hadn't bothered to tell them that, either.

Jess wasn't sure what made her angriest: the fact that Luke had dumped his dog, or the fact that he'd put her in an impossible position. She didn't want to look after his dog, but she had no way to refuse. Not without explanations she didn't want to make, because she'd had enough of people pitying her.

'He needs a lesson in manners,' she said to the dog. 'And a lot of lessons in how to look after you. You haven't even got any toys to keep you busy.'

The dog shifted closer to Jess and put her head on Jess's knee.

Jess had to fight back the tears. It'd been so long since she'd worked at a desk with a dog cuddled up close to her. And the spaniel-shaped hole in her life felt as if it had just opened up again.

She dragged in a breath. 'Let's see what we can sort out for you, sweetie.' A word with the catering department netted her a plastic bowl for water, and a word with the props department gained her a tennis ball. 'It's a bit sketchy, but it's better than nothing,' she said. 'We'll work round this.'

And she wouldn't bond with the dog in just one day.

Would she?

That, Luke thought as he headed for the temporary building of the production office, was possibly one of the worst days he'd ever spent in his entire career as a film actor. A co-star who wanted to be treated as if she were the empress of the entire universe, a ridiculous bill for replacing a pair of shoes that said co-star could barely walk in, and now he had to go back and collect the dog that had been dumped on him. The dog he didn't want. The dog who'd wrecked both his house and his sleep over the last two days.

The icing on the misery cake now would be another of those snide little articles asking if Luke McKenzie was in the process of making another box office flop. He was pretty sure that the last couple had been written by one of his ex-wife's cronies, but calling them both on it would just result in yet more bad publicity for him. Say nothing, and he was a wimp. Protest, and he was a spiteful bastard who was trying to get revenge on his ex. Whatever he did, he lost.

'Just grin and bear it,' he told himself. Fleur would get over the guilt eventually, and she'd stop trying to paint him as the bad guy in an attempt to make herself feel better about what she'd done.

He hoped.

There was *one* way Luke could turn the tables on her and get all the sympathy, but he wasn't prepared to do that. Particularly as he knew how quickly the press could put the opposite spin on a story to get more mileage from it. That part of his life was private, and it was staying that way.

OK. He only had to put up with the dog until Thursday. Just another three days. Then his aunt would be back in London to find the dog a permanent home; and he could get back to concentrating on his career. And on making damn sure that this movie was a huge success so Fleur and her cronies wouldn't be able to say another word.

Luke walked into the office, expecting to see Ayesha Milan, but the only person he saw was the new assistant. He hadn't actually caught her name this morning. He really regretted that; he'd always sworn that he wouldn't be one of the stuck-up stars who forgot what it was like to be at the bottom of the heap. He usually made a point of making sure that anyone who worked with him knew that he appreciated what they did and he didn't take them for granted. Today, he'd slipped up. Badly.

'Mr McKenzie,' she said, her mouth thinning. 'Come to collect your dog?'

'Yes.'

He was about to apologise for the way he'd dumped the dog on her that morning, but she didn't give him the chance. 'I don't care if you're Mr Big Shot Actor, and I don't care if you complain to Ayesha and get me fired for this, but what you did this morning is most definitely *not* the way to treat a dog. You dumped her on us—without any water, any food, any bedding, any toys—and that's just not good enough.'

OK. He already knew that.

She wasn't finished. 'My sister and my best friend think you're the greatest as a movie star.'

Implying, he thought, that *she* didn't.

'But, let me tell you, you totally suck as a dog owner.'

He couldn't deny that. She was speaking the truth.

'Absolutely. I know nothing about dogs.' He paused. 'And Baloo isn't mine.'

That seemed to take the wind out of her sails. 'She's not yours?'

'I'm looking after her—not that I had any

choice—until my aunt gets back from America in three days' time.'

'Oh.' She paused, frowning. 'Why didn't you have a choice?'

'Doesn't matter. I'll take her off your hands, now.' Not that he was going to make a good job of it. The next seventy-two hours or so were going to stretch him to the limit. It didn't help that the dog had chewed his script, too. The damned dog chewed *everything*. Worse still, how could he remain angry with an animal who leaped around in joy and wagged her tail madly when she saw him, and right now was sitting at his feet, looking up at him with what was definitely the canine equivalent of a dopey welcoming smile?

'Why didn't you have a choice?' The assistant's voice was softer, now. Kinder.

God, how easy it would be to let himself respond. But he couldn't afford to do that. He needed to keep his focus.

'Your aunt must've known you're working this week. She could've booked Baloo into kennels.'

'She's not my aunt's dog, either.' The words slipped out before he could stop them.

She raised an eyebrow. 'So how come your aunt asked you to look after Baloo?'

It was a long, long story.

Diversion was the best tactic here. He smiled at her. 'I'm sorry; I didn't catch your name earlier.'

'Jess Greenacre.'

'Jess.' Short for Jessica? A staccato name, clipped and a little harsh. How she'd been with him when he'd walked in. But now he looked at her—Jess. Softer. Sweeter. She wasn't wearing a scrap of make-up, not even mascara to enhance those amazing green eyes.

And what the hell was he doing, letting himself notice that? He shook himself. Even if he was in a position to think about another relationship, it sure as hell wouldn't be with anyone remotely connected to the movie business. Been there, done that, and been vilified by the press for it. Which really rankled, considering that he hadn't been the one who'd cheated and broken up the marriage.

Though he *had* lied. About one tiny little fact. And if that ever got out…

He shook himself. 'Jess. I was pretty short with you this morning. Rude, even. I'm sorry. This is your first day on set, isn't it?'

She looked surprised that he'd noticed. 'Yes, it is, Mr McKenzie.'

'Call me Luke. And welcome to the team,' he said.

She folded her arms. 'OK, you get points for good manners. Even though I suspect you might be acting your socks off, right now.'

To his surprise, he found himself laughing.

When was the last time he'd really laughed like that? Really been amused?

And when was the last time someone had called him on his behaviour instead of tiptoeing round him? Probably not since before the break-up of his marriage.

Jess Greenacre was refreshing. And she was the first person in a long while to intrigue him. She looked older than the average production assistant, so this probably wasn't her first job. So why was she in such a junior role?

None of his business, he reminded himself.

'I'm not acting right now,' he said. 'And I'm not usually—well, like I was this morning.'

'But your dog had just chewed your co-star's shoes, there were some feathers that needed unruffling, and time was tight. You were under too much pressure, and you snapped.'

She'd worked all that out? Bright as well as refreshing, then. Apart from the one thing she just hadn't seemed to grasp. 'Baloo's not my dog, but otherwise yes,' he admitted. 'My co-star didn't want a doggy audience at rehearsals. I did put Baloo in a crate but then she howled the place down and the director wasn't too pleased. I thought she'd be OK if I let her out. She sat really nicely and just watched. I thought it would be fine.' He sighed. 'I wasn't prepared for her to sneak off when my back was turned and steal some shoes to chew. Even though she's pretty much destroyed my house, the last two days.'

'Destroyed your house?' Jess asked.

'I left her for ten minutes on Saturday morning to get some croissants and a newspaper. She opened every cupboard in the kitchen while I was gone and shredded every bag and box she could find. You wouldn't believe how much mess rice, pasta, oatmeal and a bag of flour can make. Or how long it takes to clear up.'

Jess raised an eyebrow. 'You didn't leave her with any toys?'

'She didn't come with toys.' He sighed. 'She's gutted three cushions, shredded two newspapers, chewed my script—and she can undo doors, so she won't stay on her own bed at night and then insists on having more than half of mine.'

This time, Jess laughed. 'I think Baloo needs something to keep her mind busy. Like those balls you can stuff with treats, and the dog has to work hard to get the treats out.'

Jess sounded as if she actually knew what she was talking about. 'You know stuff about dogs?' he checked.

She looked wary. 'A bit.'

'Jess, I need help. I know *nothing* about dogs. I've never had one.'

'So why did your aunt ask you to look after her?'

'It's a long story.' He looked at her. 'You've probably been in here since the crack of dawn, and you'll be expected in at the same time tomorrow. I can't hold you up any longer. That's not fair. I'll take the dog and let you get on.'

She looked surprised, as if she hadn't expected him to notice the kind of hours the production team worked. And he could hardly blame her. She'd accused him of acting like Mr Big Shot Actor.

Which, admittedly, he had.

'I'm not usually this much of an idiot,' he said. 'Without a good support team, no matter how many awards the cast has won between them, a film just won't happen. You need the whole crew to work together, whether they're in front of the camera or behind the scenes.'

'Right.' She looked thoughtfully at him. 'I

can stay a bit longer. How about I make us a cup of tea and you tell me about Baloo?'

'How about,' he said, '*I* make the tea?'

'But you're—'

'Part of the team,' he cut in, not wanting to hear her repeat that he was Mr Big Shot Actor. 'If you're going to tell me things that can help me deal with a shoe-stealing dog who chews anything she can get her paws on, then making you a cup of tea is the very least I can do.'

Was he still acting? Jess wondered.

Then again, Ayesha had said that Luke used to be a total sweetheart, but he'd had a hard time over the last year and it seemed to have changed him.

Maybe this man was the real Luke Mc-Kenzie, rather than the arrogant, grumpy man she'd met this morning.

And everyone deserved a second chance.

Well, *nearly* everyone. There were a couple of people that Jess hoped would stay in prison for the rest of their lives. Though now wasn't the time to think about that.

'Thank you, Mr McKenzie.'

'Luke,' he reminded her.

This was surreal. Since when would an A-list movie star ask you to call him by his first name? She pinched herself surreptitiously, just in case this was some weirdly realistic dream. It hurt. Not a dream, then. 'Luke,' she repeated. 'I like my tea very weak and milky.'

'So the tea bag says hello to the water and disappears again? That's utterly gross,' Luke said, 'but OK, if that's how you want it. Sugar?'

'No, thanks. Tell me about Baloo.'

'My aunt volunteers at a home for abandoned dogs,' he said. 'Baloo was—um—oh, just cover her ears for a second, will you?'

Cover the dog's ears? Jess didn't get it, but she did as he asked.

'She was on death row. Monica—my aunt—smuggled her out. The problem was, Monica had to be at the airport six hours after that, and all the kennels were full.'

Jess smelt a rat. A very, very big one. *'All* the kennels were full?'

'According to Monica, yes. She didn't actually tell me why Baloo was on death row, but I'm guessing it's to do with the stealing and chewing.'

'Normally it's because they're an older dog who's been abandoned, or because the owners can't look after them any more—' Jess forced herself not to think *because they'd died* '—and none of their friends or family has room for a pet. She's young and healthy.' She shrugged and stopped covering Baloo's ears. 'You're probably right about the chewing. I'd guess it's separation anxiety, especially as she wanted to be with you and she doesn't cope with being left alone. But your aunt must've realised you know nothing about dogs.'

'Yeah. Half the time, I'm not even in London; having a pet wouldn't be fair because it would spend half its time in kennels.'

'But you still agreed to look after Baloo.'

'Temporarily. We're rehearsing this week, and Monica's back the day we start shooting.' He raked a hand through his hair. 'I had no idea that looking after a dog would be this hard.'

'A dog who's been kicked out of at least one home, to be on dea—well, in the position she was,' Jess amended. 'A dog with special needs. Not the easiest starter dog for a rookie owner.'

'You know about dogs.' It was a statement, not a question.

A lie would be too obvious. 'Yes.'

'Can you help me?' he asked. 'Please? I know you're a virtual stranger and I have no right to ask you for help, but apart from my aunt you're about the only person I've met who knows anything at all about dogs.'

Which wasn't her problem. She could just walk away. This wasn't part of her job description. She didn't *have* to deal with the dog.

But Jess had never been the sort to walk away and refuse help when someone needed it. Saying no would be denying who she was.

'Please, Jess?' he asked again.

'You're the star of a movie, where I happen to be the production assistant and I'm supposed to do whatever I'm told. All you have to do is tell Ayesha you want me to jump, and she'll ask you how high,' Jess pointed out.

He winced. 'God. I always swore I'd never be like that. And I was horrible, this morning. Worse than Mi–' He stopped abruptly.

Jess could guess whose name he'd just cut off. Mimi, his co-star. Owner of expensive designer shoes, and clearly also hater of dogs.

'I'm sorry,' he finished.

She was pretty sure now that he wasn't acting. His eyes were almost silver in this light. And they were utterly sincere. 'Maybe you were having a bad day,' she suggested.

'A lot of bad days all in a row,' he said, wrinkling his nose. 'But that's still no excuse for treating people badly.'

Did he have any idea how cute it made him look when he wrinkled his nose like that?

Yes, of course he did. He must do, she thought. It was his job, after all. Hunky movie star. The job description no doubt included the line: *must look gorgeous and appealing to all women at all times.*

'Jess, can you help me? Please?' he asked again.

More charm. He'd made her a cup of tea, just the way she liked it. And she noticed how often he'd used her name—a trick she'd been taught at work, too. It made people have confidence in you if you used their name. It made them feel that you were on their side. It made whatever you said feel *personal.*

No.

She ought to say no.

She didn't want to get involved with another dog. Not after losing Comet. The whole point of working as a freelancer was that she wouldn't get time to bond with any of her colleagues—not like her days with the police, when she knew every single dog in her team and every single handler she trained. When they were friends as well as colleagues. When she'd known most of the dogs from the moment they were born.

Being that close to everyone had left her

life in tatters, and she just couldn't let that happen all over again.

'Please, Jess?' he asked softly. 'I can't hold up rehearsals until my aunt gets back. We're on a tight schedule and a tight budget as it is. And I definitely can't take Baloo back to the dogs' home. You know what will happen if I do.'

The dog would be put down.

And Jess had had enough death in her life, this last year or so. She couldn't bear the idea of a young, healthy dog being put down just because she hadn't been trained and was a bit boisterous.

'She needs training. Which means a lot of time and hard work and patience,' Jess warned.

'I guess that'll be Monica's job. Or maybe when she gets back she'll find the right home for her, with someone who can do the training. But for now Baloo's with me. And I haven't got the time to train her or give her the attention she needs.' He stooped to scratch the back of the dog's head, and the dog rubbed her face against his knee.

Not his dog, hmm? From Jess's point of view, that looked like some serious bonding going on. He'd made a fuss of the dog without even realising he was doing it. And the dog was looking adoringly back at him. As far as Baloo was concerned, she'd found the person she wanted to live with for the rest of her days; Jess had a feeling that Luke might not have quite as much say in the matter as he thought he did.

'So can you help us, Jess? Please?'

Say yes, and open herself up to the risk of getting involved and being hurt.

Or do the sensible thing and say no, sorry, she couldn't.

Except that would mean refusing to help a dog who was already in trouble and had nobody to speak up for her. How could Jess possibly do that?

'Can't you find a dog-sitting service?' she asked in a last-ditch effort.

'Dump her on someone else, you mean?' He grimaced. 'Monica trusted me with her, and I've already messed up once. I feel Baloo ought to stay near me.'

'Even though you keep telling me she's not your dog?' She couldn't help calling him on the inconsistency.

'Fair point.' He sighed. 'Look, Monica's my favourite aunt. And she's batted my corner more than once. This is my chance to do something for her. I just need someone to help me get through the next three days.'

Three days.

Knowing that she was probably doing totally the wrong thing, but not being able to steel her heart enough to be sensible, Jess said, 'OK. I'll help. Provided it's OK with Ayesha.'

'Thank you, Jess. I really appreciate this.'

When Luke shook her hand, it made Jess feel all funny. Tingly. Weird. Like nothing she'd ever experienced before.

Then again, Luke McKenzie was a movie star. He had stage presence—no, *screen* presence—and this was a straightforward case of being faced with that for the first time. After a couple of weeks of working on the set, no doubt she'd be completely immune to it.

'No problem, Mr McKenzie,' she mumbled.

He gave her another of those knee-melting smiles. 'I meant it when I said to call me Luke.'

Oh, that smile. On the big screen, his smile was stunning. In real life, it was a hundred times better. No wonder he had a ton of female fans willing to fall at his feet and do just about anything for him. Jess was horribly aware that she'd just joined their ranks and she understood now for the first time why her sister and her best friend had always raved about him so much.

Because Luke McKenzie really was something else.

'So, where do we start?' he asked. 'What time are you in tomorrow?'

'Half past seven.'

'You'll need time to get stuff sorted, first. Shall I meet you here at half past eight?' he asked.

Again, Jess's whole body felt tingly and weird. Which was crazy. Luke McKenzie wasn't asking her out on a date and arranging when and where to meet her. Of course a movie star wouldn't ask an ordinary person on a date. He just wanted her to help him train his dog. This was business.

'If it's OK with Ayesha,' she said again.

'If what's OK with me?' the production manager said, walking back into the office and clearly overhearing the end of Jess's words.

'I need help with the dog,' Luke said. 'So she doesn't steal anything else from Mimi and chew it to pieces. It's only for three days. And I'm more than happy to pay for a temp to fill in for Jess.'

'Baloo wasn't any trouble today,' Jess said. 'I don't need anyone to fill in for me. I can still do what I need to do here and have her with me.'

'Are you sure?' Luke asked.

She nodded.

'If the actors are happy, then I'm happy,' Ayesha said. 'OK, Mr McKenzie. Jess can help with your dog.'

He grimaced. 'We were on first-name terms when we worked on *A Forever Kind of Love*, a couple of years back. Or would you prefer me to call you Ms Milan now?'

Ayesha winced. 'This film isn't the same as that one.'

'You mean, *I'm* not the same,' he said softly. 'I'm sorry. I shouldn't take my personal life out on my colleagues. You're right—I haven't been my normal self on set for a while now, and that isn't fair to the rest of the crew. Let me know if I've upset anyone here, and I'll have a quiet word with them and apologise tomorrow.'

Ayesha nodded. 'Thank you, Luke. That makes things a bit easier.'

'And I'll try not to be such an idiot in future.'

That earned him a lick on his hand from Baloo, and Jess couldn't help smiling.

Maybe she wasn't doing the wrong thing, agreeing to help.

Maybe this was going to be just fine.

And maybe, she thought, Baloo was going to do them both a favour. Help them both move on from a difficult situation in the past.

'Half past eight,' he said to Jess.

She nodded. 'Bring her water bowl, food bowl and whatever she eats during the day, a bed and some toys.'

'Toys?'

'Baloo, you need to take him shopping,' Jess told the dog. 'Something to chew is top priority.'

'Not squeaky,' Ayesha called over, 'or you'll drive me potty.'

Jess laughed. 'There you go, Luke. Your mission, should you choose to accept it…'

He laughed back. 'That's about right. OK. Doggy toy shop it is, then. Come on, Baloo.'

CHAPTER TWO

AT HALF PAST seven the next morning, Jess was in the production office, running errands for Ayesha and sorting out all the things that needed to be done before rehearsals for the day started.

It still didn't feel real that she was meeting Luke McKenzie this morning.

And she still wasn't quite sure whether he was a genuinely nice guy who was struggling through a tough time, or arrogant, selfish and just playing Mr Nice Guy in order to get her to dog-sit for him.

Either way, she needed her head examining. Spending a day with a dog was the last thing she needed.

But at least today she was prepared. And she had every intention of making Luke McKenzie do some of the work.

At twenty-five past eight, he turned up with the dog and several bags. 'Morning, Ayesha.

Morning, Jess,' he said as he walked through the door.

'Morning, Luke,' Ayesha said.

'Good morning, Luke,' Jess echoed. 'And hello to you, Baloo.'

The dog wagged her tail madly and strained on her lead, pulling Luke along the length of the office to get to Jess, and then put her paws on Jess's knee and licked her face.

'Get down, you bad hound,' Jess said, but her tone was very far from scolding.

She'd missed this so much, having a dog around.

But she knew she had to compartmentalise. This was a job.

Three days.

No bonding.

'I've just ticked the last thing off your list. Is it OK for me to go and help train the dog for an hour or so, Ayesha?' Jess asked.

The production manager looked up from her desk. 'Sure.' She smiled. 'I'll have another list waiting when you get back.'

'That's fine,' Jess said.

Luke produced a box of expensive-looking chocolates and handed them to Ayesha. 'Thank you for lending me your assistant. She'll be back with you as soon as we start rehearsing.'

Ayesha went pink with pleasure. 'Dark chocolates. How lovely.'

'I hope I remembered right?' he checked.

'Oh, you did—dark chocolate's my absolute favourite.' She smiled at him. 'Thank you, Luke. See you both later.'

A showy gesture from a movie star? Jess wondered. Or a heartfelt thanks, and he'd actually taken the trouble to remember the production manager's tastes? Or maybe it was a mixture of the two, because people were never quite that simple.

'Right. One bed, one water bowl, one food bowl, one doggy packed lunch, one non-squeaky bone to chew, one ball, one rope thing...' Luke handed Jess the contents of the large bag, one by one.

'What, did you buy up the whole pet shop?' she asked, amused.

'No. I stood in the doorway with Baloo and asked the assistant to get me stuff to keep a chocolate Labrador from chewing everything in sight. Oh, and I said it had to be stuff with no squeaks.'

Jess looked at the assortment of toys on her desk and grinned. 'I think you've just about got enough to keep her interested.'

'I hope so,' he said, sounding heartfelt. 'So what are we doing this morning?'

'We need a quiet corner to work in. No distractions for Madam, here,' Jess said, unable to resist scratching the dog behind her ears. Baloo closed her eyes in bliss.

'A quiet corner. Let me think for a second. OK.' Luke took them to a bit of the set Jess hadn't been to while running errands the previous day.

'The very basics are "sit" and "stay". I'd guess that Baloo's never been trained at all, so it might take her a while to pick it up,' Jess warned. 'Baloo, sit.'

The dog glanced at her blankly.

Jess gently stroked down the dog's back. 'Baloo, sit.'

The dog sat; Jess gave her a piece of chopped liver from her pocket and the dog wolfed it down before licking her hand in gratitude.

'Dog treats?' Luke guessed.

'Cooked chopped liver,' Jess enlightened him.

'And you keep it in your pocket?' Luke looked horrified.

'In a Ziplock bag. But, yes—if I left it all within her reach she'd scoff the lot within seconds and I wouldn't have any training treats left,' she pointed out.

He eyed her curiously. 'You've done this before, haven't you?'

There was no point in lying. 'Yes.'

'So, if you can train dogs, why are you working as a temporary production assistant?'

Because I can't handle doing my old job.

'It's a job.' Jess shrugged. And, to stop him asking any further questions, she said, 'Right, your turn.'

It took him a couple of goes, but Baloo sat for him.

'Now the treat.' Jess offered him the bag. Was he going to be all prissy about it and refuse to get his precious movie star fingers dirty?

But he took a piece of liver from the bag and gave it to the dog.

That was a good start, she thought. Maybe she could work with him.

'Next, we teach her to stay.' She got Baloo to sit. 'Stay,' she said, and walked a couple of steps away.

Baloo bounded straight over to her, clearly panicking that Jess was going to leave.

'No, sweetheart, I'm not going anywhere. But I need you to do what I tell you,' Jess said. She walked Baloo back to the spot and tried it again. On the fourth attempt, the dog got it. 'Good girl.' Jess made a fuss of her and gave her a treat.

'Your turn,' she said to Luke.

Again, it took a couple of tries, but eventually the dog did what he asked. 'Good girl,' he said, and made a fuss of her before giving her a treat.

Luke didn't seem to be so uptight today, Jess thought. He was definitely more relaxed than he'd been yesterday, and he was interacting with the dog instead of dumping her as fast as he could on someone else. Maybe it was because rehearsals hadn't started yet today, so he hadn't had to deal with his difficult co-star; or maybe the dog was helping him relax.

She so wanted it to be the latter.

They worked with the dog for a bit longer before the runner came over. 'Mr McKenzie, the director's ready for you now.'

'Sure,' he said with a smile. 'I'm coming now. Jess, thank you—and you're sure it's OK to look after Baloo today?'

No, she wasn't sure at all. 'Ayesha said it was OK.'

He pulled a wad of paper from the back of his jeans, ripped a corner off one piece and scribbled a number on the back. 'Any problems, this is my mobile phone.'

Luke McKenzie was giving her his mobile phone number?

Surreal.

It was a far cry from her old life.

She stopped the thought before it could grow any more. The past was the past, and she couldn't change it. There was no point in dwelling on it and wishing, because doing that hadn't made a scrap of difference in the last year. The shooting had still happened, the drug-dealers were all still in jail with life sentences, Matt and Comet were still buried under a carpet of flowering bulbs, and she still had nothing left but memories and wishes.

'I can hardly ring you in the middle of rehearsals. It'd mess everything up.'

'Text me, then. I'll leave my phone on silent,' he said.

'OK.'

Back in the production office, as promised, Ayesha had another list ready. Jess worked her way through it, either at her desk with Baloo snuggled in her bed next to Jess's desk, or with the dog by her side as she walked round the set, taking scripts to people and running errands.

'So what did you do to Luke McKenzie to

make him human again?' Ayesha asked when Jess returned from the last errand on her list.

'I told him what I thought of him,' Jess confessed. 'Sorry.'

'That's a dangerous tactic, Jess. If he'd been a certain other member of the cast—one who cannot *possibly* be named—then you would've had to grovel publicly and you would still have been fired,' Ayesha said. She came over to make a fuss of the dog. 'But well done. It's nice to see Luke being more like his old self. Let's hope it lasts.' She looked at the dog. 'She's beautiful, isn't she? And she's the perfect match for him. Sexy movie star hero with the cute dog. How could any woman resist that combination?'

Good question. Well, Jess would have to, for her own peace of mind. She wasn't looking for a relationship. Even if she was, she knew that Luke McKenzie was from a different world—one where she wouldn't fit in. She was ordinary, and he lived his life in the glare of the spotlights.

'Time for your lunch break, I think. Though you'll need to take the dog with you.'

'Sure.' Jess smiled at her boss and then looked at Baloo. 'How about a run in the park opposite?' she asked Baloo.

The dog looked at her as if she was speaking Martian.

'Your owners didn't do that with you, did they?' She sighed. 'OK. Walkies?'

Baloo still looked blank.

'You're going to enjoy this, sweetie,' she said. 'But I'd better let Luke know where we're going.' She didn't want to call him, in case he was in the middle of a scene; but she was pretty sure a text would be safe and he'd be able to pick up the message later.

She texted Luke to tell him she was taking Baloo to the park, put the dog's water bowl in a bag, then headed off the set.

When Jess took Baloo for a run, she realised how much she'd missed it. Working out on a treadmill in a featureless gym was nothing like running outside in the fresh air, with grass and trees all around, and the scent of spring blossom in the air. There really was nothing like running with a dog bounding along by your side. She swallowed hard. It wasn't the Labrador's fault that her head was still a bit messed up. But the memories made her catch her breath and she had to stop.

She filled the dog's water bowl from the bottle she carried with her, then bought another bottle of water from the kiosk in the park, along with a chicken wrap for her lunch.

Once she'd settled herself on a park bench and Baloo was sitting next to her, the dog looked hopefully at her. Or, rather, at her chicken wrap.

'You think I'm going to share this with you?' she asked.

The dog's expression was eloquent enough, and Jess laughed. 'OK. You can have some of the chicken, but I'm going to make you work for this, Baloo. Shake hands.'

To her surprise, the dog caught on very quickly. What a shame that her former owners hadn't seen her potential. And what a shame that Baloo was only going to have a temporary home with Luke McKenzie.

Maybe she could…

No. She stopped her thoughts before the temptation got too strong.

Her lease said no dogs—and that was one of the reasons why she'd chosen the flat in the first place. To make sure that she had a solid reason not to weaken and let another dog into her life. A dog she could lose, the way she'd lost Comet. She'd spent the last year putting the pieces of her life back together, and the only way to keep herself safe was to keep herself separate. She needed to remember that. She absolutely couldn't adopt Baloo. No matter how tempting the idea was.

* * *

Luke checked his phone during the scene break. There was a message from a number he didn't recognise; he assumed it was from Jess and flicked into it.

She was taking Baloo to the park?

That was definitely above and beyond the call of duty. He still felt a bit guilty about dumping the dog on her, but what else could he have done? He couldn't leave Baloo at home because he knew she'd trash the place and he didn't want the dog in a situation where she could get hurt. He couldn't take time off from rehearsals, because that wouldn't be fair to the rest of the cast. And, thanks to Mimi's tantrum after the shoe episode yesterday, he couldn't keep the dog on the set with him either.

And then there was Jess herself. Straight-talking, and not afraid to stick up for an unwanted dog even if it could mean she'd be fired.

Something about her drew him.

Which was ridiculous. Apart from the fact that Luke wasn't in a place where he was even looking for a relationship, for all he knew Jess could be happily married, or at least committed to someone. Even if she wasn't, who would want to date a man in the public eye and have her life stuck under the less than kind microscope of the press? And when Fleur's cronies found out he was dating her, they'd rip her to shreds in the press. He couldn't let that happen. And that meant keeping some distance between them. Not acting on the attraction.

He texted back:

Enjoy the park. Will be rehearsing until about five. Let me know if any problems. And thank you.

A few moments later, his phone beeped to signal an incoming message. Jess again.

All fine. Baloo v keen on chicken.

Uh-oh. Had the dog stolen her sandwich? Something else he'd have to replace.

He typed:

Sorry. Will reimburse you for anything Baloo steals or trashes.

The reply was a smiley face.

No need. Is training aid.

'Luke, we're ready to go again,' the director called.

Director wants me back to work. See you later.

He switched his phone off again when the message had been sent.

At quarter to six, Luke walked into the production office. 'Sorry I'm late. Rehearsals overran a bit.'

Jess looked up from her desk and smiled. 'No worries.'

At the sound of his voice, Baloo leaped up from her bed, woofed, and raced over to him.

'I think someone's missed you,' Ayesha said with a grin.

'Just tell me she didn't disgrace herself,' Luke said, rolling his eyes.

'She's been great,' Jess told him. 'Actually, Baloo has something she wants to show you. Stand in front of her and crouch down a bit. Baloo, shake hands,' she instructed.

The dog obliged by lifting her paw and shaking hands with Luke.

'Wow. I didn't know she could do that.' He looked impressed.

'She can now. She picks things up quickly

and Labradors are very trainable—I think you could have a potential movie star dog here.'

He laughed. 'If I didn't know better, I'd say my aunt called you and recruited you to her campaign to get me a dog.'

'She adores you.'

'Because I'm her favourite nephew. Yeah, yeah.'

'I meant the dog adores you.' Jess couldn't help laughing. 'You're that used to people adoring you?'

'My aunt, yes.'

Interesting that he'd mentioned his aunt rather than his parents or grandparents. So did that mean he was closer to his aunt than to any other relative? Had he lost his parents young, maybe?

Not that it was any of her business. She was simply looking after his dog for three days, not becoming his best friend or anything even close to it. She needed to back off. Now. 'I, um, guess I'd better let you and Baloo get on,' she said. 'See you tomorrow.'

'OK. Want me to make you a cup of tea before I go?' he asked.

Ayesha coughed. 'How come you've managed to snag yourself a personal tea boy, Jess?'

Luke grinned. 'If I remember rightly, Ayesha, you hate tea and only drink espresso. Stronger than anyone else I know can take it, and that includes the Italians.'

'Actors and their memories. I swear they have elephant genes,' Ayesha teased.

'Well, there has to be some benefit to learning lines,' Luke said with a wink.

'Jess, you can go now, if you like,' Ayesha said. 'I'll finish up here.'

'Sure?' Jess asked.

'Sure,' Ayesha confirmed.

And somehow Jess found herself walking out of the office with Luke McKenzie.

'Can I take you for a drink to say thank you?' he asked.

Now she knew he was being polite. And she'd be polite back. 'Thanks, but no. I have a standing date on Tuesday evenings.'

'Uh-huh.'

'With my sister, my best friend and a pizza.' And why had she felt the need to explain that? she wondered, cross with herself. He wouldn't be interested. He was a movie star, for pity's sake, not a normal everyday guy.

'Enjoy,' he said. 'Maybe we can take a rain check on that drink.'

A permanent rain check, she thought. So they'd never actually go. 'Sure.'

'Seriously. Baloo and I owe you.'

A mad idea floated into her head. 'If you really want to say thank you, you could give me two signed photos.'

He looked taken aback. '*Two* signed photos?'

What, did he think she meant to sell them on eBay or something? 'For my sister and my best friend,' she explained. 'It'd make their day. They drag me off to see all your films.'

He grinned. 'Under duress, would that be?'

She winced. 'Sorry, that came out wrong. I like your films, too.'

'But rom-coms aren't your thing?'

'I like them,' she said, trying to be polite.

'But?'

'But I prefer action films,' she confessed. 'Especially sci-fi. I'm sorry. I don't mean to be rude.'

He laughed. 'No, it's refreshing. It's nice to have someone being honest instead of telling me that they've seen all my films twenty times and I'm the best actor in the world—which I know I'm not. Of course I'll give you a signed photo for your sister and your best friend. It's the least I can do. Come back with me and Baloo to my trailer and I'll get them now.'

'You have a trailer? And one of those chairs with your name on it?' She felt her eyes widen. Luke McKenzie was a huge international star, and he'd made her feel so at ease that she'd actually forgotten that.

He laughed again. 'Don't be expecting a huge palace with gold-plated taps or what have you. It's just an ordinary caravan. Somewhere to have some space to myself.' He scratched the top of the dog's head. 'Which Madam here would chew up in a matter of seconds if I left her there.'

Baloo just gave him an innocent look.

Jess followed him back to the trailer. As he'd said, it was just a caravan, a place where he could make himself a drink and chill out. It was also incredibly tidy; either he was a neat freak, or one of the runners had to tidy it up for him every day. There was a dog cage, she noticed; obviously the one he'd talked about yesterday, from which the dog had escaped.

'Photos. OK. Give me a second.' He rummaged in a drawer and brought out two photographs and cardboard envelopes. 'Who do I sign them to?'

'Carly—she's my sister—and Shannon, my best friend, please.'

He took out a pen, signed the photographs with a flourish, and put them neatly in the envelopes.

'Thank you.' She smiled. 'You'll probably hear the shrieks of joy all the way across London when I hand them over tonight.'

'Pleasure.' He rubbed the dog's ears. 'Right, you. Home for dinner. And don't keep me awake tonight with your snoring.' He rolled his eyes. 'I had no idea that dogs snored. Or that they were pillow hogs.'

'Oh, they snore, all right. And they'll sneak onto the sofa between you if they think they can get away with it.'

He glanced at her left hand, and she realised what she'd just let slip. Cross with herself, she lapsed into silence.

It sounded very much to Luke as if Jess Greenacre had once had a dog, but didn't have one any more. And she'd also clearly been in a relationship, though she wasn't wearing a wedding ring.

So what had happened?

Had it been a bad break-up and her ex-partner had claimed custody of their dog? Was that why she'd been reluctant to look after Baloo, because it brought back memories of a dog she missed very badly?

She clearly didn't want to talk about it because she'd gone quiet on him and the laughter had gone from her green eyes.

Luke was shocked to realise that he wanted to make her smile again. Which was crazy; he didn't plan to get involved with anyone, ever again. Fleur had put him off relationships for life. Picking up the pieces when things went wrong was hard enough; to have to do it in the full glare of the media spotlight had been a nightmare.

But he couldn't leave it like this, with things so awkward between him and Jess. The best way he could think of to break the ice again was to ham it up. Entertain her. 'And she raided my shoe rack. She had one of every single pair in her bed yesterday, didn't you, Madam?'

The dog glanced up at him and looked as if butter wouldn't melt in her mouth.

Jess reached over to rub the top of the dog's head. 'That explains a lot.'

'Does it?' Luke was mystified.

'I think I can tell you her history now,' Jess said. 'She was left home alone a lot. Her owners probably weren't used to dogs and either didn't know how to train her or just couldn't make the time.' For a second, she looked angry—on Baloo's behalf, Luke thought. 'If they'd looked on the Internet, they could've found tips to help. Leaving the radio on, putting a blanket or an old towel in the laundry basket overnight and then putting it on her bed so it smelled of them and made her feel less alone, or giving her a special toy to distract her.'

Luke wouldn't have had a clue about any of that.

'She probably chewed the place down from a mixture of boredom and anxiety.' She sighed. 'Some people just shouldn't have dogs.'

Including me, Luke thought.

'She's really worried about being left alone, now, and she's going to need separation training.'

'That's what you said before. Is that difficult?' Stupid question. Especially as it would probably make Jess think that he wanted to learn how to do it so he could keep the dog himself. Which he couldn't.

'Not so much difficult as the fact that it takes time,' she said.

'Which I don't have.' He grimaced. 'Without you, we'd be totally stuck. And it's a relief not to have someone complaining about her all the time.'

'People whose shoes she chews?' Jess asked archly.

'I don't think Mimi minded so much about the shoes as, um, not getting time with me on her own.'

She flushed. 'Sorry. I didn't mean to get in the way of your date.'

'Trust me, I'm not dating Mimi, and I don't want to.'

'She's really that difficult?'

The look of shock on Jess's face told him that she hadn't meant to blurt out the question. 'She's really that difficult,' he confirmed wryly. 'I'm looking for an easy life right now.' Just so Jess knew he wasn't hitting on her.

'Look, I don't want to put my foot in it, but I, um, saw the papers last year.'

Hadn't everyone? Fleur had turned the end of their marriage into a total media circus.

'I get where you're coming from and, just so you know, I'm not going to turn into your Number One Fan and stalk you or anything,' Jess finished.

'I know.' He tried for lightness. 'Otherwise I'd set my dog on your shoe wardrobe.'

'Shoe wardrobe?' She looked surprised.

'Don't all women have them?' he asked. Fleur had needed a walk-in wardrobe to hold all her shoes—organised by colour and heel height. She'd had ten pairs of black court shoes with four-inch heels, and Luke hadn't been able to tell the difference between them.

'I have three pairs of shoes,' Jess said. 'No, *four*, if you count my running shoes.'

He laughed. 'I like you. You're refreshing.'

'Thank you. I think.' She smiled, and it sent a thrill all the way down his spine. Which was crazy. He and Jess came from different worlds. He barely knew her. He couldn't be reacting to her like this.

'Just for the record, I think I like you, too.' Then she grimaced. 'Sorry. You must hear that all the time, people coming up to you and telling you they love you.'

He smiled. 'It happens a bit, yes, but I'm not daft enough to think that they love *me*. They don't know me. They love the character I played in a movie, and there's a big difference between the two.' Which had been half the problem with Fleur. She'd loved who she thought he was, not who he really was. That, and the fact that he hadn't been able to give her what she really wanted.

'I suppose it's like the baddies in soap operas. People shout at them in the street because they confuse them with the character, and they might be incredibly sweet in real life instead of being mean,' she said thoughtfully. 'So you're not a handsome, charming and posh Englishman with floppy hair, who isn't very good at talking about his feelings?'

He laughed. 'Got it in one.' Though, actually, he knew it wasn't that far off the mark. He'd been typecast for a reason. 'Well—I'd better let you get on. Enjoy your evening with your sister and your best friend.'

'I will, and thanks again for the photos. Enjoy your evening, too.' She made a last fuss of the dog. 'And you, be good. We'll do some more training tomorrow. And go for another run.' She glanced at Luke. 'She likes running, by the way. And there's nothing like a good run with a dog at your side.'

'If that's your idea of a subtle hint,' he said, 'I'd hate to know what a heavy one's like.'

'You want a heavy hint?' She laughed. 'When you've had a day of dealing with people you have to be civil to, but really you want to shake them until their teeth rattle and tell them to grow up… That's when a good run with a dog at your side will definitely put the world to rights. Even if you do have to go out in public wearing dark glasses and a silly hat.'

'I do not wear dark glasses and a silly hat,' he said.

She folded her arms. 'My sister gets every magazine with your picture in it, so I know you're not telling the truth. You've got a silly hat. A beanie. I've seen it.'

'Busted,' he muttered, enjoying himself hugely. When had he last met someone he could have fun with like this?

'I think you should steal the hat, Baloo,' Jess said in a stage whisper. 'Chew it to pieces. Then he'll have to go and get a sensible one.'

Luke couldn't remember when he'd enjoyed bantering with someone so much, it had been so long ago. 'What counts as sensible? Deerstalker? Fez? Top hat?'

She groaned. 'You're not Sherlock Holmes, Dr Who or Fred Astaire.'

'Ah, but I'm an actor,' he said. 'So I *could* be. If you wanted.' He did a little tap dance. 'See? I'm Fred.'

She grinned. 'Don't make me dare you.'

'Dare me,' he said softly, willing her to dare him to kiss her. Because right at that moment, he really, *really* wanted to kiss her.

But then panic flared in her eyes, as if she realised that their flirting was starting to get a bit too intense. A bit too close. 'I need to get going. See you tomorrow. Bye, gorgeous.'

The way she made a last fuss of the dog made it clear to Luke that the 'gorgeous' had been directed at the Labrador, not at him.

Pity.

He was definitely attracted to her. He thought it might even be mutual. But to act on that attraction would be the most stupid thing either of them could do. They were from different worlds. It would never work. And if it turned out that she, like Fleur, wanted something he most definitely couldn't provide…

Better not to start anything he couldn't finish. 'See you tomorrow,' he said. And watched her walk away.

CHAPTER THREE

JESS'S ENTRY-PHONE rang at precisely seven-thirty. She buzzed her sister and best friend up, and met them at her front door with a hug.

'Pizza,' Shannon said, waving the box at her.

'Wine, strawberries and ice cream,' Carly added, handing over the pudding. 'And we want to know *everything*.'

'Food first.' Jess shepherded them into the kitchen, where the table was already set, and put the strawberries in the fridge and the ice cream in the freezer.

Carly poured the wine. 'So how was it?'

'Fine.'

'Brave face fine, or *really* fine?' Carly persisted.

'Really fine,' Jess reassured her with a smile.

'So tell us all about it. What's it like, working on a film set? Did you see anyone famous?' Carly asked.

'Set rules—everything's confidential. So I can't tell you that much about it,' Jess warned.

'Confidential. Just like your old job,' Shannon said wryly.

No. Because this time Jess wasn't getting involved. And nobody was going to get hurt. Working on a film set was nothing like being a police officer, apart from her work having to be confidential. There were no thugs with loaded guns to face, for starters. It wasn't life or death. 'Not quite. Everyone I worked with was nice.'

She couldn't tell Carly and Shannon everything about Luke McKenzie—if she told them about Baloo, she knew they'd both suggest immediately that she should move to a flat that allowed animals and give the Labrador a home. But she was looking forward to their reaction to her little surprise. 'As for anyone famous… You have to keep this totally confidential, OK?'

'Promise. Cross our hearts,' they chorused, following up with the actions.

'Good.' She fetched the cardboard envelopes and handed them over. 'These are for you.'

She watched the expressions on their faces

as they opened the envelopes and took out the signed photographs. Surprise turned to disbelief and then delight—and then the pair of them hugged her half to death.

'Oh, my God. You met Luke McKenzie! I can't believe it. My little sister just met the most gorgeous man in the world. What's he like?' Carly asked.

'Complicated,' Jess said. 'When I first met him—well, he was being Mr Big Shot Actor.'

'But he's always so nice in interviews,' Shannon said, looking disappointed.

'He got a bit nicer as the day went on,' Jess said.

'Maybe he's just not a morning person and needs a ton of coffee before he's even halfway human,' Carly suggested. 'I still can't believe you actually met him.'

'Is he as beautiful in real life as he is on the screen?' Shannon asked.

More so. But Jess couldn't quite admit to that. It would be totally inappropriate to have a crush on Luke McKenzie. She was the most junior member of the film crew, and he was the headline actor. 'You wouldn't be disappointed,' she said.

'So you're actually working with him?' Shannon shook her head. 'Wow. I can't take this in.'

'He's not the only actor in the movie,' Jess said with a smile.

Carly laughed. 'You're talking to *us*. Of course he's the only actor in the movie!'

Jess laughed back. 'Come on—let's eat before the pizza gets cold, and I'll tell you as much as I can about today.'

At the end of the evening, Carly held her close. 'It's good to see you smile again, Jessie,' she said. 'I know you've had a really tough time of it, this last year, and it's been hell watching you go through it and knowing that I couldn't do anything to make things better for you. I would've given anything for a magic wand to fix things. I still wish I could bring Matt and Comet back. Well, not even have them in danger in the first place.'

'You were there for me, and just knowing that I could call you at stupid o'clock in the morning if I needed to helped a lot,' Jess reassured her.

'You never actually called me, though,' Carly pointed out. 'Because you're too stubborn.'

Jess gave her a rueful smile. 'I guess I just needed time to come to terms with things in my own way. I'm never going to stop missing Matt and Comet, but I'm finally learning to see the sunshine again.'

'I just wish you'd go back to working with dogs,' Shannon said. 'You loved your job so much. And working as a temp doesn't make you anywhere near as happy—even if you did get to meet the most gorgeous man in the world today.'

'I'm fine,' Jess said. She'd heard this argument countless times before. And she had the same answer: she wasn't ready to go back to working with dogs. She might not ever be ready. As a temp, she kept her days too full to think, and that suited her right now. 'See you both later. Text me to let me know you're home safely.'

'Of course,' they said, rolling their eyes.

She couldn't even use the excuse that she was a policewoman any more. She just wanted to know that they were safe. *Needed* to know.

'Stop worrying, sweetie,' Shannon said and hugged her. 'Everything's going to be just fine.'

On Wednesday morning, Jess spent an hour working through Ayesha's list, then had an hour of training with Luke and Baloo before his rehearsals. She was guiltily aware that her best friend was absolutely right about Jess being happiest when working with animals:

despite her initial reservations, Jess was really enjoying training the dog. She loved seeing the Labrador blossom and become more confident as her training progressed. And she'd missed this.

Maybe she should consider going back to it. Not with the police—she knew she couldn't handle the idea of training people and their dogs to face the kind of situation Matt and Comet had faced—but maybe she could set up classes doing something like this. Or even working with the animal handling department of a film company.

'She's doing really well,' Luke said. 'I can't believe how quickly she's picking things up.'

'She's very trainable. And this will make her life easier.' Jess paused. 'And yours.'

'Baloo's not mine,' Luke reminded her.

Oh, yes, she most certainly is, Jess thought, but kept her counsel.

As the runner came up to tell Luke that the director was ready for him, Jess said, 'See you later. Break a leg—or is that only said for stage performances?'

He laughed. 'It's pretty much the same thing. Thanks, Jess. See you later.'

At lunchtime, Jess's phone rang.

'Hi. It's Luke,' he said.

As if she wouldn't recognise that voice—like melted chocolate, warm and rich and sensual. 'Hi.'

'I was wondering if you and Baloo would like to have lunch with me.'

'Baloo's very partial to chicken sandwiches,' she said. 'So if they're on the menu, our answer is yes.'

He laughed. 'I'll bear that in mind. See you at the catering tent in ten minutes, then?'

'Hang on, I'll just check with Ayesha.' When the production manager confirmed that it was fine for Jess to take her break, she told Luke, 'Yep. Ten minutes.'

And hopefully by the time she met him her common sense would be back in control. Along with her knees, which right now were doing a great impersonation of blancmange. Ridiculous. Luke McKenzie was a movie star. He was *supposed* to have that effect on women. It wasn't real.

They reached the catering tent at practically the same time.

'The team here is pretty good,' Luke said. 'I don't know if chicken sandwiches are on the menu today, but I can definitely recommend their BLTs.'

Baloo looked hopefully at him, and Jess

laughed. 'Bacon is full of salt. Which is not good for dogs.'

Baloo hung her head and looked sorrowful.

Luke ruffled her fur. 'Did you train her to do that?'

'No. She's a natural.'

'Don't say it,' Luke warned, 'because it's not going to happen.'

Jess spread her hands. 'Not a word will pass my lips.' But she was thinking it, and she knew he knew it.

'So how was your pizza last night?' he asked as they walked over to the catering area.

'Good. I meant to say earlier, my sister and my best friend asked me to say thank you for the photos. They were thrilled.'

'My pleasure,' he said simply.

The bacon, lettuce and tomato sandwiches were as good as Luke had promised. Although Jess refused to let Baloo have any, she relented enough to let the dog have a treat from her pocket, and the dog settled between them both with a happy sigh.

'Care to indulge a nosey actor?' Luke asked.

Her heart skipped a beat. 'How?'

'Set rules,' he said. 'Were you a dog trainer before you did this job?'

Apart from the last year. But she wasn't going into that. 'Pretty much,' Jess said. 'I thought about being a vet when I was at school, but I realised I couldn't handle the tough side of it—situations where I couldn't make an animal better and had to put them down.' She grimaced. 'I was never allowed to watch Lassie films as a child because I'd always sob through them.'

'I was never allowed to watch them, either,' Luke said.

Jess had hoped he'd be soft-hearted when it came to animals. Good. Things were starting to look that much more hopeful for Baloo.

'So what made you think of being a trainer?' he asked.

'I took my dog to agility classes when I was twelve, and I loved it—I got chatting to the trainer, and she suggested it,' Jess explained. 'My parents were brilliant and supported me all the way. I did a degree in animal behaviour, then qualified as a dog trainer.' Luke didn't need to know that she'd become a police dog trainer and had spent two years as a police officer first.

'So what made you stop?'

My husband and my dog were shot and killed. That was a tricky one to broach. And she didn't want Luke to pity her and treat her like a special case. She grimaced. 'Right now, do you mind if we don't talk about it?'

'Sore spot?' he asked.

She nodded.

'Sorry.'

'Not your fault.' Taking the focus off herself, she asked, 'What about you? Did you always want to be an actor? Obviously, that's under set rules.'

'Sure.' He smiled. 'Actually, I read law at university,' he said, surprising her. 'I was meant to join my dad in the family firm.'

Clearly that hadn't happened, or they wouldn't be on the film set together right now.

'Then I joined Footlights,' he said.

She blinked as his words sank in. 'You were at Cambridge?' So he was super-bright as well as gorgeous.

He gave a self-deprecating shrug. 'I loved Footlights. I met some really nice people—people who are still close friends now—and found what I really wanted to do in life.'

But he'd just told her that his family had expected him to follow in his father's footsteps. Had they been disappointed when he hadn't? Or had they encouraged him to follow his dreams? Jess wished now that she'd paid attention whenever Carly or Shannon had thrust a magazine article about Luke McKenzie in front of her. It would be rude to ask him, and she could hardly grill her sister or her best friend—not without giving an explanation she wasn't ready to give. So she just smiled at him and hoped he'd take it as an invitation to continue talking.

'I had a deal with my parents that I'd take a year out after graduation. If I couldn't make it as an actor within that year, then I'd join the family firm and train as a barrister.'

'I think you'd have made a good barrister,' she said. 'You've got presence and that would show in court.'

'Thank you.' He looked at her, his eyes narrowed slightly. 'That sounds as if you're talking from experience.'

She backtracked fast. 'I know a couple of barristers,' she said, keeping it vague. He didn't need to know that she knew them professionally rather than socially. 'So obviously you made it as an actor.'

'By the skin of my teeth—half the time in that first year I was "resting" and working as a waiter,' he admitted. 'It got to the eleventh month in my year out and my parents were starting to put pressure on me—but then I got my lucky break. A director had seen me play Benedick in *Much Ado* and wanted me for the lead in her new film. It was a small-budget indie production, and it was pretty likely that it wasn't going to get anywhere, but I loved the script. So I thought I might as well end my acting career doing something I really loved.'

'Was that when you played Marcus Bailey?' It was the film her sister and best friend had first seen him in and fallen in love with him. Thousands of other women had clearly felt the same, because the independent film had taken the world by storm. 'That was the one.' He smiled. 'Which is why I'd work for free for Libby. Without her I would've been stuck in chambers. I mean, I could've done the job, and I would've put in enough effort to make sure I did it well—but I would always have regretted losing my dreams.'

Her own parents had always been so supportive, Jess thought. She'd been really lucky. Whereas Luke's parents had given him an ultimatum and put pressure on him not to follow his dreams. She wondered if his aunt Monica—the dog rescuer—had been the one to take his part. Though asking wouldn't be tactful. Instead, she turned the conversation to something much lighter, and by the time they'd finished their sandwiches his laughter was definitely genuine and showed in his eyes, rather than being faked to put her off the scent.

'Has anyone told you how restful you are?' Luke asked when they'd finished.

Jess looked surprised. 'How do you mean?'

'You don't need to fill all the silences.'

She shrugged. Probably because she was used to spending her time with animals. You needed to know when to shut up and let them get on with their job. 'Is that so unusual?' she prevaricated.

He laughed. 'I guess I hang around with too many actors. They're not so good at shutting up.'

'But you use silence in films—for comic timing and what have you.'

'That's scripted,' he said. 'Or your own interpretation of the script. That's different. I mean outside work. And it's so nice not having someone trying to set me up on a date.'

'Tell me about it,' she said, rolling her eyes. 'They've found absolutely the *perfect* partner for you, so all you have to do is go on a date with them and life will be fantastic again.'

'You, too?' he asked.

She wrinkled her nose and nodded, and Luke wondered if she knew how cute she looked.

Probably not.

There was nothing studied about Jess. What you saw was what you got. She wasn't like most of the women in his world, very aware of how every move and gesture could be interpreted.

'Not everyone tries to fix me up,' Jess said. 'My parents, my sister and my best friend know I'll date again when I'm ready.'

'And the others?'

'Have discovered that I'm not very available.' She wrinkled her nose again. 'Which is horrible of me. I know they mean well and they want me to be happy.'

'But you'd rather choose your own date.'

She nodded. 'You, too?'

'You're lucky that your family understands and doesn't push you,' he said feelingly. 'I've pretty much run out of excuses to avoid my mother's dinner parties.'

'Tut, and you an award-winning actor.'

Luke couldn't remember the last time he'd met someone with such a dry sense of humour. Someone who made him laugh for all the right reasons. He grinned. 'You have a point. If I can't act my way out of a dinner party, I shouldn't be doing this job.' He scratched behind Baloo's ears, and the dog sighed with happiness. 'Like you say, they mean well and they want you to be happy.

But sometimes their idea of what makes you happy isn't the same as yours.'

'So you still miss Fleur?' She grimaced. 'Sorry, that was really nosey. I shouldn't have asked you. Ignore me.'

'It's OK.' Of course she'd be curious. And of course she'd know his ex-wife's name. The gossip pages had been full of their divorce, last year.

'No, it's not OK,' she said. 'You don't have to tell me.'

Luke was surprised to find that actually he did want to tell her. Some of it, anyway. Jess might be the one person who really understood how he felt. And he already knew he didn't have to remind her about set rules. What he said to Jess would stay with her and go no further.

'Sort of. I know I don't feel the same way about her as I did eighteen months ago. I don't love her any more.' He didn't hate her quite so much any more, either, so that was progress. Of sorts. 'I suppose I don't miss *her* so much as I miss being married,' he said. 'I miss the closeness.'

She nodded. 'Yeah. That's the hard part. Waking up in the middle of the night and the bed feels too big.'

She definitely knew what he was talking

about, then. 'It's the stupid little things. Putting the kettle on to make tea and remembering that you only need one mug. Buying croissants for one at the deli on a Sunday morning.'

'Coming home, and there's nobody to tell about your day—because if you ring someone to talk about it then they'll know you're feeling lonely and miserable. Then they'll feel bad if they can't change their plans and come and see you; and you'll feel bad if they *do* come and see you, because you know you really ought to be able to cope with it on your own,' she said.

Oh, yes, he knew that one, too. 'Then, the next day, they'll ring you and suggest joining them for dinner or a show at the theatre or the opening night of an exhibition, and you go along to discover they've also invited someone else—someone they think might stop you being lonely.'

'And you're polite, and you try to have a nice time, but it pushes you even further into that little box of loneliness,' she said.

'Absolutely.' He reached over and squeezed her hand. 'Thank you.' Her skin was soft and warm, and he had to resist the temptation to draw her hand up to his mouth and fold a kiss into her palm. Which would be insane, because that wasn't what either of them wanted. She was offering him friendship. Understanding. And that was exactly what he needed, right now. He loosened his hand from hers. 'You have no idea how good it feels to meet someone who understands that.'

'Me, too,' Jess said.

'I'm glad I met you.'

'And you.' She smiled. 'If anyone had told me six months ago I'd start to make friends with a movie star, I would've—' She spread her hands, laughing. 'Well, I don't move in those sort of circles.'

'You do now.'

She laughed again. 'I'm hardly Hollywood material. I don't think I'd fit in.'

He thought that Jess would fit in just about anywhere. But now wasn't the right time to say that. 'Hollywood's a lot of pressure.' He shrugged. 'And a lot of relationships can't take that. I thought Fleur and I would buck the Hollywood trend—that we'd be one of those strong marriages that can survive one of us working away for half the year. I loved her and I thought she loved me.' Except she hadn't loved him enough. She'd wanted something he hadn't been able to give her—at least, not something he could give her easily, and how she wished he'd been able to do it. But a simple childhood illness had put paid to that. Somehow they'd managed to keep that little bit of information out of the press. But the nasty little secret had been eating away at him ever since. Along with the fear that it would be leaked. And that it would change people's view of him—and in turn that would change directors' views of him, too, and mean that he wasn't considered for the role of romantic male lead any more. Actors in the Fifties had had to keep their sexuality under wraps for the same reason: public perception could close off huge areas of their career. Nowadays, it was acceptable for an actor to be gay. But Luke's problem was a little tricky.

'I'm sorry it didn't work out that way for you.'

'Me, too. But she's with someone else now.' Someone who *had* been able to give her what she wanted. Which was how he'd learned about her affair in the first place.

Jess reached over and squeezed his hand. 'Sorry. I didn't mean to bring back bad memories for you.'

'Not so much bad memories as regret,' he said. 'I wish things could've been different. But they're not, and I've pretty much learned to come to terms with it.' He blew out a breath. 'Thank you for not pitying me.'

'Pity's harsh.'

It sounded as if she was speaking from experience. He wanted to ask, but he didn't want her to go back into her shell. If she wanted him to know, she'd tell him. 'Yes, it is,' he said, leaving it up to her whether or not she wanted to talk.

'I hated it when people pitied me—or people crossed the street to avoid me because they didn't know what to say to me. They'd pretend later that they hadn't seen me, but I knew they had.'

'People always take sides in a breakup,' he said. 'You can't always choose your friends.'

'No.' She looked away.

'I'm not going to pry,' he said.

'Thank you.'

Her words sounded heartfelt. Clearly she still loved the guy who'd broken her heart. Maybe it hadn't been as long for her since the breakup as it had for him; he'd gradually trained himself to stop loving Fleur. Except he was aware that it had also made him keep an emotional distance from anyone he'd dated, too. Or maybe he just hadn't found the right person to help him to trust again.

Like Jess. And Baloo.

He pushed the thought away. He wasn't getting involved. End of story.

'That's me back on set,' he said regretfully when there was a call for his scene. 'I'll see you later. Have a nice afternoon.'

'You, too. Break the other leg,' Jess said. 'Baloo, wave goodbye.'

To his surprise, the Labrador sat and put her paw up, for all the world as if she were sketching a salute goodbye. 'Wow. You taught her that?'

She grinned. 'This morning, in a quiet moment in the office.'

'You,' Luke told the dog, ruffling her fur, 'are a very clever girl.' He looked up at Jess. 'And you might be a genius.'

'It's all her. Sweet-talk your director and get her a part in his next film,' Jess said with a saucy wink. 'See you later.'

That wink stayed in Luke's head all afternoon, to the point where it even distracted him from some of his lines. Which really wasn't good. He was a professional. He never let things put him off his stride at work.

This was crazy.

He couldn't be attracted to Jess Greenacre.

He didn't want a relationship. He was pretty sure that she was in the same position; she was guarded about her personal life, and something major had clearly happened in her last job to make her change direction so completely in her career. But the little that she had let slip made him think that she was recovering from a broken relationship and needed time to get her head together, too. She was the worst person he could get involved with.

Enough.

He had work to do.

He made it through the first scene without letting himself think about Jess. And the second. But, in the short break after the second scene, Mimi sashayed across to him. Wearing the expensive designer shoes Luke had replaced the day before.

'Hey, Luke.' She gave him a sultry look to accompany the equally sultry drawl.

'Hey, Mimi.' He forced himself to be charming. He was going to have to work with the woman for the next couple of months, and the last thing the rest of the cast needed was any awkwardness between the lead actor and the lead actress.

'I was thinking, maybe we could have dinner tonight.'

Her pout made it very clear that dinner wasn't all she planned to offer. Oh, help. Everyone knew he was single, which probably made him fair game in his world. But even if he had been interested in a relationship, Mimi wasn't his type. Too mannered, too studied, too fake. Every move was calculated for maximum effect—and maximum PR. If he dated Mimi, the pictures would be plastered all over the gossip magazines, the very next day. And he'd had quite enough of his personal life being in the press, thanks to his ex-wife.

'Sorry, Mimi. I'm already promised elsewhere tonight,' he said, giving her an equally fake but absolutely charming smile, and hoping that would be enough.

'Tomorrow night, then. To celebrate the first day of shooting.'

'Sorry, no can do—my aunt's back tomorrow and she'll need a proper update on Baloo.'

Mimi's smile slipped just a fraction and her eyes went cold. 'The mutt.'

'Actually, Jess thinks she's a pure-bred Labrador.'

'Jess? Oh, yes. The *gofer*.' The actress made it sound as if Jess were the lowest of the low.

Shockingly, Luke found himself wanting to defend Jess. Which was crazy. She was perfectly capable of standing up for herself. Plus, if Mimi thought he was taking Jess's part over hers, she was capable of making life very difficult on set for Jess. Best to back off. Discretion being the better part of valour, and all that.

Though at that precise moment Luke thought he was as much of a coward as Shakespeare's rotund knight. Maybe the easy life wasn't necessarily the best life.

'You're sure you can't get out of your plans tonight?' Mimi asked, giving him another of her famed sultry looks. 'You can't throw a sickie?' She dipped her head and looked up at him, making her blue eyes seem huge and pleading. 'Not even for me?'

'Sorry, Mimi. No can do.' He knew he needed to keep this polite and firm, without giving any explanations that could give her an excuse to prolong the conversation or try a different tack. 'I don't know about you, but I could really do with a coffee. Shall we join the others?'

To Luke's relief, the actress agreed. And George, the director, had clearly seen his predicament and taken pity on him, because he needed a quick chat with Luke alone about tweaks to the last scene.

'You know, Mimi usually dates her leading men,' George said quietly.

Yeah. Luke knew. But he didn't want to

date her. 'I'm not in the market for dating, right now,' he said.

'Just one date, for a quiet life,' George suggested.

It would be the easy way out. But Luke couldn't face it. This wasn't a game he wanted to play.

And he was horribly aware that if Mimi was a different person—a gentle-voiced woman with intelligent green eyes, no make-up and a sharp sense of humour—then the situation would be very different.

'Maybe I can persuade her that I'm still not over Fleur,' he said.

'Well, you can try,' George said, his expression saying very clearly that he thought Luke would need to be very lucky indeed for it to work.

CHAPTER FOUR

LUKE TRIED TO ignore the noise, but the shrilling was insistent.

Then his groggy brain focused on the fact that it was the telephone.

In the middle of the night.

Nobody called him at this time of night. Not unless it was an emergency.

He groped for the receiver, his eyes still not accustomed to the low level of light in the room, and mumbled, 'Hello?'

'Lukey, it's me.'

He registered firstly that it was his aunt Monica, and secondly that her voice sounded gravelly, as if she'd been crying. And then he was wide awake. He switched the bedside light on, trying to dispel the flood of panic. 'Monica? What's happened? Are you OK?'

There was a quiet woof from the end of the bed, where Baloo had settled herself—Luke had given up trying to make her sleep in her crate in the kitchen.

'Not really.' She dragged in a breath. 'I can't believe I was so stupid. I've broken my leg in two places.'

'Where are you?'

'Hospital. Laura's with me.' She paused. 'Oh, no. You were asleep, weren't you? I got the time difference wrong. I'm so sorry.'

She sounded very, very close to tears. 'It's fine, Mon,' he reassured her. 'You know you can always call me at stupid o'clock if you need me. That's what family's for.'

'Thank you, love.' She choked back a sob. 'They won't let me fly home tomorrow. And I promised I'd be back and I'd rehome the dog for you.'

There was another gentle woof from the end of the bed.

'Did I just hear her bark?' Monica asked.

'Uh, yeah.' He raked a hand through his hair. 'Let's just say Baloo's good at opening doors and I've given up trying to make her sleep downstairs.'

Monica gave a huff of laughter. 'That's the first thing I've heard all day to make me smile. It's been a rotten day, Lukey.'

'What happened?'

'We were hiking. We'd gone to see the falls.

I slipped and landed awkwardly.' He could practically hear her inject a note of bravery into her voice. 'It's just one of those things.'

'You said you broke your leg in two places.' So it must've been a pretty nasty fall. And if she'd been out hiking… 'How did you get to hospital?'

'A combination of the mountain rescue team and an ambulance. Luckily I've got decent travel insurance,' Monica said lightly. 'And good painkillers.'

Considering that his aunt didn't even take paracetamol for a headache, that told him a lot. 'How long are you going to be in hospital?'

'I don't know. They want to make sure there aren't any complications, and the cast has to set. I don't know when I'll be able to fly. And—oh, Lukey, I've let you down. I'm supposed to be in London, not stuck in Portland.' She sounded anguished. 'Are you all right to keep Baloo until I get back?'

Keep the dog for an unspecified length of time—which could mean anything from a couple of days to a few weeks, depending on when his aunt was able to fly home again and how mobile she was.

No, he wasn't all right to keep the dog. He had a film to shoot. The deal was, he'd look after the dog until the end of rehearsals. Monica was supposed to pick up the dog on Thursday afternoon. *This* afternoon.

But his aunt was clearly in pain and upset. Luke wasn't mean-spirited enough to make her feel guilty about the change in plans on top of all that. 'It's fine,' he lied. And he just hoped that Jess would be able to help him out. He had no idea how long her contract was with the film company—a week, a month, the whole of the film—but she'd been a dog trainer. Maybe she knew someone else who could step in, if she couldn't do it.

'Mon, is Laura still with you?' he asked, not wanting to think that his aunt was alone and in pain.

'Yes. She's going to change her flight and stay here with me, at least until we know what's happening.'

'Good.' Though he knew he'd be happier if he saw his aunt for himself. Laura was one of Monica's closest friends, but there wasn't quite the same bond as there was with family. And Luke was the nearest Monica had to a child. If he was honest with himself, he was closer to his aunt than he was to his parents. 'Look, I can head to Heathrow now and get the next flight over. Tell me which hospital you're in and which ward, and I'll get a taxi from the airport when I land.'

'No, love. You're shooting the film this week. You haven't got time to fly halfway across the world.'

That was true. But family was more important. He'd find some way of sorting this. Maybe the director could shoot out of order and do some of the scenes Luke wasn't in, tomorrow. Half a day's filming—it could be done, he was sure. 'For you, I've got time.'

'Lukey, don't. I'll start crying.' She sniffed. 'Really, I'll be fine. Don't go to the airport. You'd better get back to sleep. You'll have bags under your eyes tomorrow and your director will want to strangle me.'

'No, he won't. The make-up team is pretty good,' he said with a smile. 'Don't worry. Do you have your mobile phone or is there another number I should use to call you?'

'There's a phone next to the bed. I think I'm meant to keep my mobile off. Do you have a pen?'

'Give me a second.' He grabbed a pen and scribbled the phone number on the back of his hand as she dictated it. 'I'll call you tomorrow morning.' He chuckled. 'That's tomorrow your time, I mean—it'll be afternoon here when I call.'

'I *am* sorry I woke you, Luke. I wasn't thinking straight. I just—' Her voice caught. 'I just wanted to talk to you.'

'Don't worry about it, Mon. It's not every day you break your leg.' And, although his aunt packed more into her life than anyone else he knew, she was a lot closer to sixty years old than to twenty. A fall and broken bones were bound to shake her up, and he knew that it would take her much longer to recover physically than if she'd been his age. 'Ask for anything you need and I'll pick up the bill, OK? Just remember that nothing's too much trouble or too expensive when it comes to my favourite aunt. Anything you need, you get it. I mean it.'

'Thank you, Luke.' She sounded close to tears again. 'I love you.'

'Love you, too, Mon. Get some rest and I'll call you tomorrow.' He put down the receiver. *I love you.* Monica was the only person in his life who said that to him and meant it. He blew out a breath. And how pathetic was he for minding? Anyone would think he was five years old again, not thirty-five. He'd minded then. He knew better now.

'Get a grip, McKenzie,' he told himself roughly. He was doing just fine. He had a good career, plenty of friends and a comfortable house. He didn't need anything else.

During the conversation, Baloo had moved further up the bed and had curled up by his knees.

'It looks as if you're going to be my house guest for a bit longer,' he said, stroking her head.

She licked his hand.

'It's still only temporary,' he warned her. 'Just until Monica's leg has healed. And then she'll find you a real home.'

Another lick.

'And we'd better hope that Jess can help us out. Otherwise you and I are going to be grovelling to Mimi for *weeks*. We're talking flowers every day, shoe-shaped chocolates, and more charm than I'm capable of.'

Baloo put a paw over her nose, and he laughed. 'I think Jess is right. You could be a showbiz dog.' He stroked her head. 'But I can't keep you. It wouldn't be fair to either of us.'

She just looked at him.

'I can't.' And he wasn't going to think about how much he'd bonded with her in the few days he'd been looking after her—especially since he'd been working with Jess to train her. How much he was enjoying having company at home. How good it was to let himself care about someone again.

To Luke's relief, Jess was already in the production office when he and Baloo walked in the next morning.

And he was aware that it wasn't just relief that she'd kept her word about helping out with Baloo. Jess's sweet, shy smile made the world feel as if it was a brighter place. Which was crazy. He'd only known her since Monday. Less than a week. Although she was looking after his dog while he was rehearsing, they were still virtually strangers. He couldn't possibly start feeling this way about her. He didn't want a relationship with her— with *anyone*.

He made an effort to control his thoughts. 'Good morning, Jess.'

'Good morning, Luke.' She bent to make a fuss of Baloo. 'It's your last day with Baloo and the first day of shooting today, isn't it? Do you have time to do any training with her?'

'Yes and no.' He wrinkled his nose. It wouldn't be fair to let Jess look after Baloo all day and then drop the bombshell on her that he needed her help tomorrow as well—and probably for quite a few days after that. 'Can we have a quick chat in my trailer, first?'

She looked surprised, then a little wary, but nodded. 'Sure. What's up?'

'Tell you when we get there.' He didn't want to have this conversation on the open set and then have everyone gossiping about him. Been there, done that, and rather not rinse and repeat.

Once they were in the trailer, he unclipped Baloo's leash from her collar and the dog settled down on the rug. 'Can I get you a coffee or anything?' he asked.

'No, I'm good, thanks.' Jess frowned. 'What did you want to talk to me about?'

'My aunt called me in the middle of the night,' he said. 'From America. She's in hospital.'

Jess looked shocked. 'Oh, no. What happened?'

'She was out hiking when she had a fall. She broke her leg in two places, so they're keeping her in for a few days. She was meant to be arriving home this morning and picking up the dog this afternoon, but right now I have no idea when she's going to be allowed to fly home.' He grimaced. 'It might not even be until her leg is healed. Which could take weeks.'

'It depends on the length of the flight, her age, and how bad the break is,' Jess said, surprising him. 'Do you know how long the flight is?'

'She's in Portland—I think she said it was something like eleven hours between there and London.'

'So she'll need to get up and move around a few times during the flight, then. With a cast, she's more of a risk of developing DVT,' Jess said thoughtfully.

'How do you know this sort of thing?' Luke asked.

She shrugged. 'I used to know a few medics. It kind of rubs off.'

He was intrigued. Why would a dog trainer know medics? But he had a feeling that she'd clam up on him if he asked. Besides, he had a more pressing question.

'As I said, I don't know how long it's going to be before Monica comes back to London. But, even once she's home, she's not going to be able to look after Baloo with a broken leg,' Luke said. 'It's going to be hard for her even to let the dog out, and she definitely won't be able to take Baloo for walks.'

Baloo gave a soft woof, and he bent to stroke her head. 'I didn't mean now, you daft hound. She knows the W-word,' he told

Jess ruefully. 'I can help out a bit, but not enough—not when I have full days shooting on set. And I can't pull out of the film this morning, not when they start shooting this afternoon. It wouldn't be fair to the team and I can't expect someone else to come in at ridiculously short notice and learn the part.' He shook his head. 'It just wouldn't be fair on anyone. A lot of people are relying on me. I can't let them down. But I can't let my aunt down, either.' He looked at her. 'Jess, I really need your help, and I'll understand if you can't do it, but if you could help me look after Baloo until Monica's properly back on her feet...'

Look after Baloo. With Luke. Spend time with both of them. *Get close to them.*

No. Jess knew that she should walk away, right now. That would be the sensible course of action. Walk away and don't get involved.

But she had a nasty feeling that it was already too late. She'd already started bonding with the dog. And she couldn't even begin to let herself think about what was happening with Luke himself. How she'd been looking forward so much to the mornings at work because it meant spending time with him as well as with Baloo.

She was an idiot. She should know better than this. Getting involved would be a bad, bad, *bad* idea. Especially with someone who was so very much in the public eye—someone who was way out of her league.

But Baloo was looking at her with pleading brown eyes. Luke was looking at her in exactly the same way. And she was pretty sure that this was genuine, not just an actor excelling in a role.

They needed help.

From her.

Could she be mean-spirited enough to say no? Especially as working with Baloo had helped her to focus, move on to the point where she was able to think about maybe going back to her old career, albeit in a civil role rather than with the police force?

Jess took a deep breath. 'OK. I'll do it.'

Luke wrapped his arms round her and held her close. 'You're a lifesaver. Thank you so much.'

It was the first time in more than a year that a man had held Jess tightly like this, as if she were the most precious and most important thing in the world. The first time since Matt had been shot. Part of Jess wanted to bawl her eyes out, remembering how much she'd lost.

Part of her wanted to hug Luke back. And a really crazy part of her wanted to tip her head back in invitation for a kiss.

Oh, help.

This was unfair to both of them. Luke had made it clear that he wasn't interested in a relationship, and neither was Jess. This had to stop right now. She needed to be sensible. Yes, the man was drop-dead gorgeous, but she was just being star-struck. This was a re-action to stage presence or whatever it was that actors had.

'You're going to be late for work,' she said.

'I guess.' He pulled away and took a step back. And there was a slash of colour across his cheekbones that she'd never seen before.

Oh.

So did he feel this weird pull of attraction, too? She'd guess that he didn't particularly want to feel that way, either.

But they were both far from being teen-agers. So they could deal with this like the adults they were. Couldn't they?

'I'll see you later,' she said.

He nodded. 'I'll call you when we break for lunch. And thank you, Jess. I really do appreciate this.'

'No problem,' she said. 'Come on, Baloo. We're going to the office. Walkies.'

The dog perked up and wagged her tail. 'See you later, Luke,' Jess said, clipped Baloo's leash onto her collar, and headed for the production office.

Normally, Luke loved his job. He liked the script for this film, he liked the director, and he liked most of his co-stars—Mimi, admittedly, he could do without, but he'd put up with her for the sake of the film.

But today he couldn't concentrate.

All he could think about was the fact that he'd be seeing more of Jess. And how she'd felt in his arms when he'd hugged her impulsively.

It should make him want to run a mile. After Fleur, he'd dated a lot, in a vain attempt to make himself feel better. But it hadn't worked, so he'd simply stopped dating and given himself a bit of space to get his head together. He'd managed to avoid most of the situations where well-meaning friends had tried to fix him up with someone they thought would be perfect for him.

But Jess Greenacre… Jess intrigued him. He wanted to know what made her tick. What made her laugh.

She was definitely a puzzle. A dog trainer who knew barristers and medics. Or maybe they were people she'd met at university, or friends of the family, and he was making too much of it.

He just about managed to focus on rehearsals until the lunchtime break. And then he discovered he wasn't actually getting a break—they needed to go straight into shooting.

'I need to make a couple of quick calls, first,' he told George, the director.

'They need to be really quick,' George warned.

'I'm calling Jess, to let her know that I need her to look after Baloo at lunchtime, and my aunt Monica, to see how she's doing this morning,' Luke explained.

And how stupid was it that he was disappointed not to get the chance to see Jess?

'No, it's fine. I understand,' Jess said when Luke explained the situation over the phone. 'You don't need to apologise. Now go, before you get into trouble.'

In the end, she took her lunch break with Baloo in the park opposite the set. Just for fun, she ran through a couple more training moves with the dog, and was impressed by the way the dog responded. 'You could have a real career in show business, sweetheart,' she said, scratching the top of the dog's head.

Baloo sighed and rested her head on Jess's knee.

'Enough for today, I think,' Jess said. 'Give me a wave goodbye for the park?'

Baloo woofed and lifted her paw.

'That's cool,' a voice said beside her.

Jess turned to see a little girl who looked as if she was six or seven. Alone in the park and talking to strangers? That wasn't good. She tried to keep the little girl talking while she scanned the park to see if a parent or carer was nearby. Failing that, she'd put a call in to the nearest police station and get someone to look after the little girl and keep her safe until her family or carer was found. 'What's cool? That my dog can wave?'

The little girl nodded. 'Does your dog dance?'

'I've never tried dancing with her,' Jess said. Where on earth was the child's mother? Was she one of the nearby women concentrating on a mobile phone call?

'There was a dancing dog on the telly on Saturday night. It was really good.' The little girl regarded Baloo solemnly. 'You should get her to dance.'

To Jess's relief, a woman came hurrying over to them. 'Aisling! You know you shouldn't go off and talk to strangers,' she scolded, then grimaced at Jess. 'I'm so sorry. My daughter does like to talk.'

'You were on the phone, Mum,' Aisling said.

Jess schooled her face into a neutral expression, though privately she agreed with the little girl. Her mum really should've concentrated on her rather than on the phone call. Children were precious—and Jess knew from her police work how easily things could go wrong. 'Aisling, maybe next time you should wait until your mum's said it's OK before you start talking to someone,' Jess said gently. 'Not everyone's nice.'

The little girl's lower lip wobbled. 'But you've got a *dog*. That means you're nice.'

Not always, Jess thought. And the dog wasn't actually hers.

'She's desperate for a dog,' Aisling's mother explained to Jess. 'Love, you know we can't have one. The landlord won't let us have dogs because they chew things.'

'This one definitely chews and she especially likes designer shoes, which gets her into a bit of trouble,' Jess said with a smile. 'Maybe wait until you're grown up, Aisling. Then, if you can't have a dog of your own, maybe you can work with animals—you could be a dog trainer.'

'Are you a dog trainer?' Aisling asked.

It was too complicated to explain. Jess simply smiled and nodded.

Aisling brightened. 'So you *could* teach your dog to dance...'

Jess smiled. 'Maybe one day.'

She thought about it when the child had gone. Baloo had responded so well to the training they'd done so far. Would she take to performing?

She took her MP3 player from her bag, found some music, and encouraged Baloo up on her hind legs. And she was surprised by how quickly the dog picked up the idea. Two steps forward, two steps back, head to one side...

'We could work out a routine,' she said thoughtfully as she rewarded the dog for her work. 'You're the perfect dog for Luke McKenzie. I'm with his aunt, on that. You could even be in show business with him.'

Baloo's answer was to lick Jess's face, and Jess laughed.

She headed back to the production office and spent the afternoon run off her feet. Luke texted her to let her know that shooting was running over and ask if it was OK to look after Baloo a bit longer. She texted back to say it was fine, and simply carried on at her desk until he came to collect the dog.

'How's your aunt doing?' she asked.

'Better, after a night's sleep. And I told her you were helping me with the dog, so everything's fine and all she has to worry about is getting back on her feet. She still doesn't know when she'll be allowed home, though.'

Jess looked sympathetic. 'That must be so frustrating for her.'

'Given that Monica lives her life at a hundred miles an hour…I'll give her a day before being stuck in bed drives her completely crazy and she's begging to be let out.' He sighed. 'At least her best friend is with her.'

'But you'll be happier once she's back in London and you can keep an eye on her?'

Luke smiled. 'I'm not sure that Monica would allow anyone to keep an eye on her. But something like that, yes. How was your day?'

'Good, thanks.' She paused. 'Dare I ask how it's going, or is that bad luck?'

He smiled. 'I'm not superstitious. It's going OK, thanks. I'm just sorry things overran. I feel as if I'm taking advantage of you.'

She shook her head. 'It's fine. Really.'

'Can I buy you dinner?' he asked. 'Just to say thanks?'

Making it very clear that it wasn't a date, she thought. 'It's fine. You really don't have to do that.'

'Would you accept it from Baloo?' he asked.

She smiled. 'I don't think dog treats count as legal currency.'

'I'll give her an advance on her pocket money,' he said. 'Have dinner with us. It's not going to be anything fancy—I mean, I think The Ivy might just say no if I ask them to reserve a table for two and a dog bowl. But we could have some take-out in my trailer.' He nudged the dog. 'Hey. This is your cue to do the big brown eyes bit and the sad face.'

Baloo immediately dropped to the floor and put her head on her paws, looking up at Jess.

Jess couldn't help smiling. 'You two are such a double act. OK. Take-out would be lovely.'

'And it also means we won't get papped,' he said softly. 'That's the one bit I hate about my job. I don't get much privacy. I mean, yes—the film business has been good to me, and I appreciate that. I never mind spending time talking to fans and signing autographs—

without them, I wouldn't get to do the job I love. But sometimes living your life constantly in the spotlight feels like too high a price. I'd love to be able to take you for dinner at the nearest dog-friendly pub. But, if I did, there's a very good chance a photographer would be around, and then you'd find your picture in the gossip pages tomorrow morning and a lot of speculation to back it up.'

Which was the last thing she wanted. With a little bit of digging, any journalist would quickly find out that she was Matt's widow. The story would be dragged up all over again. And who knew what spin they'd use to talk about Luke?

'Agreed,' she said softly. 'At least here we're under set rules.'

'Thank you for being understanding,' he said. 'It's not that I'm ashamed to be seen with you. I mean, we're friends. And I'm not looking for a relationship right now.'

He couldn't make it clearer than that. Any secret thoughts she might've been harbouring about him—well, it wasn't going to happen. Besides, hadn't he already warned her about people who fell in love with the characters he played, which weren't necessarily anything like the man himself?

'Me, neither,' she said. Just to make sure

he didn't think that she was going to turn out to be a Kathy Bates-style 'number one fan' from the movies.

'But friends…I could use a friend,' he said.

'Me, too,' she said, and hoped her voice didn't sound as quivery as her knees felt when he smiled at her.

Luke found the menu from a local take-away online, and between them they decided on a selection of dishes.

'Can I be horribly rude and sort out a couple of things for tomorrow's filming while we wait?' he asked.

'Sure. I'll take Baloo for a walk. See you in a quarter of an hour?' she asked.

'That'd be good.'

She took Baloo into the parkland surrounding the set, and they found a patch of evening sunshine to sit in.

'I need my head examining, Baloo,' she told the dog, and was rewarded by the dog putting her paws on Jess's shoulders and licking her face.

'Very helpful,' she said dryly, making a fuss of the dog. 'If you could talk, you'd tell me that you adore him, wouldn't you?'

Big brown eyes regarded her thoughtfully.

'I think he's a nice guy. Just his life's a bit of a mess, right now. I think he needs you,' she told the dog. 'Someone to teach him to love again. To trust.'

Ha. The same could be said of her. Though she wasn't single because of a betrayal by her partner. Trust didn't come into it. Her problem was fear.

'And I have no idea how I make the fear go away, Baloo,' she said softly. 'If I let someone close…what happens if I lose them, too, the way I lost Matt and Comet?' OK, so what had happened to them was outside the norm. Death wasn't usually the result of someone's intent. It was more likely to be a serious illness, or an accident. There were no guarantees that anyone in her life could cross the road safely every day for the next fifty years. Jess knew all that, intellectually. But knowing it emotionally was a different matter. And the fear kept her shut in that box of loneliness.

'Now I'm being maudlin.' She glanced at her watch. 'And we're due back at Luke's trailer.'

They arrived at the same time as their meal. Luke found some plates and Jess served up. And then Jess fed morsels of chicken surreptitiously under the table to Baloo.

'Are you feeding that dog under the table, Ms Greenacre?' he asked, catching Jess's eye.

'Busted.' She laughed. 'Sorry, I'm really

not supposed to do that. It's a bad habit and it means she'll be a pain at the dinner table in the future, begging and expecting treats.'

'But those big brown eyes have suckered you in?'

'Yes,' she admitted.

Luke spread his hands. 'Well, she's looking for a good home. You could always adopt her.'

Jess shook her head. 'I can't have a dog where I live. Whereas I'd guess that you don't have a landlord who's banned dogs from the premises.'

He laughed back. 'Are you quite sure you haven't been talking to my aunt?'

'I'm sure.'

'Monica would like you,' he said thoughtfully. 'And you'd like her.'

'I already like what you've told me about her.' Jess ruffled Baloo's fur. 'And I like the fact that she rescued this one. Baloo's a great dog, Luke. She just gets a bit anxious when she's left, and a bit of training can sort that out. She won't always open your cupboards and chew things.'

'I guess,' he said. 'But my answer still has to be no.'

Maybe, Jess thought, he might change his

mind when he realised that Baloo was most definitely a performer's dog.

And she'd do her best to convince him.

CHAPTER FIVE

ON FRIDAY, WHEN Luke came to collect Baloo, he said, 'Jess, I know you've probably had enough of both of us this week, but would you like to have dinner with us tonight?'

Another take-out in his trailer? 'Only if it's my shout,' she said, striving for a bit of independence. She didn't want Luke thinking that she saw him as a potential open wallet. He might be wealthy, but that didn't mean he should give everyone a free ride.

'Actually, I thought maybe I could cook for us,' he said diffidently.

She looked at him in surprise. 'You can cook?'

He lifted his chin, and she was pretty sure that he was deliberately hamming up the offended expression when he intoned, 'Of course I can cook!'

'Interesting.' She raised her eyebrows. 'Considering that all the food we've eaten together since I've known you has been made by someone else—even the sandwiches.'

'It's easier that way when I'm working, because I never know when I'm going to finish,' he said, 'but, seriously, when I'm not working I usually cook for myself. It relaxes me. Come and have dinner?'

It felt like a genuine offer rather than being polite. And, given what he'd said last night, she was pretty sure he meant on a friendship only basis. 'OK, then. That would be nice.'

When the afternoon's shoot had finished, Luke drove them back to his place.

'I'm impressed that you have a crate in the back for Baloo,' she said.

'That was Monica's idea,' he admitted. 'And it's a lot easier driving her to work than dragging the poor dog across London on the Tube.'

As they drove into Bermondsey, Jess realised that they were heading towards the Thames. Did Luke actually live in a place overlooking the river?

They reached a block of modern three-storey mews houses, built from yellow brick with a line of red brick above the elegant white window frames. The ground floor of the building was painted white, to match the front door and garage doors; this was the kind of house, Jess thought, that would need a seriously large salary to support the mortgage.

Luke pressed a switch on his key fob and the garage door opened.

'Impressive,' she said. 'Parking where I live is on the street, with a permit.'

'There really isn't enough space to park on the street, here, so they built this block with integrated parking,' Luke said.

Once they were inside, he shut the garage door behind them, let Baloo out of the car, and unlocked the door to the house.

'I guess I should give you the guided tour, first,' he said, and gestured to the first two doors. 'Utility room and downstairs toilet.' He opened the third door. 'This room was meant to be a bedroom, really, but I use it as my office because of the view.'

It was incredibly neat and tidy, Jess thought. There was a very plain glass desk with a state-of-the-art desktop computer on top of it, a filing cabinet, a small sofa, and bookshelves that she itched to browse through—but she managed to stop herself, because she didn't want to appear rude and nosey.

He gestured to the French doors. 'Take a look.'

She glanced out. The room overlooked the garden and had an amazing view of the River

Thames. 'Wow—you can actually see Tower Bridge from here,' she exclaimed.

'And the City of London skyline—there's a better view from the next two floors.' He smiled. 'The important thing here is the garden, from Baloo's point of view.'

Like his office, the garden was very neat; it was laid mainly to honey-coloured paving slabs, though there were stylishly arranged terracotta pots containing flowering shrubs.

'I'm not the best gardener,' he admitted. 'The garden's all thanks to my mother. It kind of keeps her happy.'

It was the first time Jess could remember him mentioning his mother; and it sounded as if the relationship was a little strained, because he'd spoken about his aunt with a great deal more affection.

Baloo pattered up the stairs and they followed her to the landing on the next floor. 'The top two floors are bedrooms and bathrooms,' he said, indicating the stairs. 'And this is the kitchen.' It was more than twice the size of Jess's own narrow galley-style kitchen, and it looked like something from a magazine showpiece, with light ash cabinets, shiny black worktops and a slate floor. There wasn't a river view, this time, as the room overlooked the street.

Again everything was very neat and tidy; there was no clutter of any description on the worktops, apart from a kettle and an expensive Italian coffee-maker. There weren't even any magnets holding photographs or notes to the fridge. It felt like more a place to live than a home, she thought.

Not that she had room to talk. She hadn't put up any of her framed photographs in her new place, and she'd lived there for almost a year now.

The next room was a huge reception room. Again, it looked fresh from the pages of a style magazine, with soft leather sofas, a state-of-the-art TV and sound system, and what looked like original oil paintings on the wall. The floors were polished wood—clearly real wood and not cheap veneer—and there were a couple of artfully placed silk kelims between the sofas. There was an area with a dining table and eight chairs, so obviously Luke was used to entertaining.

There were two more sets of French doors on the wall overlooking the river. Luke unlocked them, and she stepped onto the narrow balcony with its wrought iron bistro table and two chairs. The view of the waterfront was stunning, and she could pick out all the landmark buildings of the London skyline along with Tower Bridge; the Gherkin and the Shard were instantly recognisable. 'This is amazing,' she said, meaning it. 'I totally get why you love this house. You can sit on this balcony and watch the world go by. Well, on the river.'

'We get some amazing sunsets with the bridge in the background,' he said. 'There are fabulous views at night, too, when all the buildings are lit up.'

'I can imagine,' she said wistfully. This was another world. How the beautiful people lived. So far from her own life. 'I can see why you chose it.'

'I wanted to live on the river, but I didn't want another flat. I wanted a house, and I was really lucky when this one came on the market.' He smiled. 'I've always liked this area of London. It has a lot of connections with film—did you know they shot part of a James Bond movie here? As well as *Bridget Jones* and *Oliver*.' He spread his hands and gave her a disarming smile. 'I can get really boring about Dickens, so shut me up when I start.'

She couldn't imagine that Luke McKenzie could be boring about anything. He had one of those voices that could make a reading of the telephone directory sound interesting— deep, clear and slightly posh. She could listen to him for hours. But obviously he expected her to change the subject, so she did her best. 'Is that the Thames Path between your garden and the river?' she asked.

'Yes. It's based on the old towpaths that the barges used,' he confirmed.

'I always meant to walk part of it—well, obviously not the whole thing.' She knew the path was almost two hundred miles long, running between the source of the Thames in the Cotswolds and the Thames Barrier outside Greenwich. 'But I never quite got round to it.' And walking it on her own, without her partner and her dog, just hadn't felt right.

'Maybe some time you could come exploring with me and Baloo,' he suggested.

Of course he'd offer. Luke McKenzie had impeccable manners. She bit her lip. 'Sorry. I wasn't fishing for an invitation.'

'I know. But I was planning to do it anyway—and, if you come with us, then people aren't going to stare at me as if I'm this total lunatic talking to my dog.'

She laughed. 'Half the time they'll be talking to their own dogs. Besides, it's more likely that they'd be staring at you, working out if they dare come and ask you for an autograph.'

He shrugged. 'Well, the offer's there. I understand if you're busy. Baloo and I have already taken up a lot of your time this week.'

No pressure. And she appreciated that. 'I'm already doing something this weekend,' she said, 'but I'd love to come for a walk with you both some time. I don't really know the Docklands area.'

He smiled. 'I do. I've lived here for five years. Well, not this house—I moved here after the divorce. There were too many memories in my old place.'

She could understand that. She'd moved out of their house a month after Matt's death, even though everyone had said she should leave it for at least three months before making any major changes in her life. But she just hadn't been able to handle going into a room and expecting to see him and Comet there, then having to relive the loss all over again. She'd needed a fresh start. Somewhere with no memories. 'I know how that feels, too,' she said softly.

'Yeah.' He wrinkled his nose. 'Time for dinner. It's a nice evening, so do you want to eat on the balcony?'

'That'd be nice. What can I do to help?'

'Nothing, really. Except maybe feed Baloo.' He showed her where the dog food was kept, and the dog sat patiently while Jess filled her bowl.

'And now for dinner.' He produced a chef's hat, making her laugh.

'No way do you wear that to cook dinner every night.'

'Oh, but I do,' he said with a grin. 'Perfect for reheating a TV dinner in the microwave.'

She laughed back. 'So do you have a full collection of silly hats, then?'

He smiled. 'Busted. Actually, I borrowed this one from Wardrobe, earlier today. And they won't be happy if I get it messy.' He took off the hat and put it safely out of the way. 'I was bluffing about the TV dinners, too. I'm not quite that bad.'

Jess watched him cook. And she noticed that he used a container of ready-prepared vegetables, another container of ready-chopped chicken, and a sachet of ready-made stir-fry sauce.

She couldn't resist teasing him. 'I thought you said you were cooking?'

'I am.'

She coughed. 'You're just throwing ready-prepped stuff into a wok and sizzling it together. That's not *really* cooking.'

He laughed back. 'It's just a quick meal. So you're a gourmet cook, are you?'

'I like experimenting,' she said. Not that she'd bothered much since Matt's death. Since then, she'd barely noticed what she ate, so there hadn't been much point in spending time on preparation.

'I think I need a demonstration. Just to prove that you can walk the talk,' he said.

Was he teasing her back, or was he serious?

She decided to call his bluff. 'Sure. I'll cook for us next weekend.' Then her common sense kicked in. She paused. 'That is, if you're not already booked up.'

'At a glitzy showbiz party?' He rolled his eyes. 'Trust me, they're not as frequent as the press like to make out. And they're even less fun.' He smiled. 'Baloo and I are free next weekend, and we'd love to accept your offer.'

Oh, help. He *had* been serious. 'Small problem,' she said. 'Not that I'm trying to chicken out. But my lease says I'm not allowed to have a dog, and one of my neighbours is a little bit…how can I put this, without being mean? I think he's lonely, so he takes a little bit too much interest in what other people do.'

'So he'll tell your landlord if you have a canine visitor, which will get you into hot water.'

She nodded. 'And you can't leave Baloo here on her own.'

The dog, hearing her name, looked up and woofed softly.

'So that lets you off the hook.'

Was that really disappointment in his expression, or was she just seeing what part of her secretly wanted to see? She decided to take a risk. 'Unless,' she said, 'you wouldn't mind me using your kitchen. Though it's a bit of a cheek to ask.'

'It's not a cheek, it's a workable solution,' he corrected. 'I'm not territorial. Though you'll have an audience when you're cooking. And we'll both expect treats for good behaviour, you know.'

She laughed. 'I love your sense of the ridiculous. Treats, hmm? I'll see what I can do.' She stroked Baloo's head. 'Talking of treats and audiences, we've been working on a little something. Would you like to see the premiere, after dinner?'

Jess Greenacre was turning out to be full of surprises. Away from the set, she was opening up more, and Luke liked the woman he was getting to know. She had a sense of fun. She teased him, and she let him tease her back. And she didn't treat him as if he were on a pedestal: she treated him like an ordinary man. Which was incredibly refreshing.

'I'd like that,' he said. 'Dinner's ready.'

He waited until she'd had the first mouthful. 'So? Cheat food, is it?'

'Yes. But it's nice. I'll give you that.'

He laughed, relaxing. And he appreciated the fact that Jess didn't have a desperate need to chatter. Silence with her was gentle, rather than awkward.

When they'd finished dinner, he let her carry her plate through to the kitchen, but refused to let her help clear up. 'That's what a dishwasher's for. I'll sort it later. You promised me a premiere.'

'I did indeed. Ready, Baloo?' she asked.

The dog gave a soft woof.

'OK. Then have a seat, sir, and enjoy the show.' She gestured to the sofa, and gave him a small bow, making him smile. Then she took her MP3 player from her handbag, flicked into a song, and set the player on his table.

He recognised the song immediately—the old classic, 'Can't Take My Eyes Off Of You'.

'I love this. It always makes me think of that movie with Heath Ledger.'

'Me, too. I loved that film,' she said, looking slightly wistful, and started the routine.

Baloo circled round her, circled the other way, then sat in front of her with her head to one side, looking adoringly at her. Luke appreciated the way Jess had matched the lyrics to the dog's actions, particularly when the dog rolled over as if her knees had gone weak, then put her paws on her nose as if shushing her words.

As the chorus began, Jess knelt in front of the dog, who sat up and then played pat-a-cake with her paws against Jess's palms, in a perfect rhythm to the song.

At the end, Baloo put her paws on Jess's shoulders and licked her nose. Jess hugged the dog. 'Good girl. You were brilliant.' She fed the dog a treat, and Baloo wagged her tail happily.

Then she shifted round so she was facing Luke. 'Did you enjoy it?'

He blew out a breath. 'More than enjoyed it. That was stunning. I can't believe you've taught her that in only a couple of days.'

'It's still a bit rough round the edges.'

'Even so, that's an amazing achievement in such a teensy amount of time.' He shook his head, impressed. 'You're an incredible trainer.'

'Baloo's an incredible dog,' Jess corrected. 'She picks things up quickly—when Monica gets her a family, it needs to be one who'll take her to something like agility classes or do this kind of training with her. I guarantee she won't chew, because she won't be lonely or bored if you keep her active like this.'

'She's really blossomed.' He drummed his fingers thoughtfully on the arm of the sofa. 'You ought to show this to my director.'

'Maybe.' But Jess looked pleased and her cheeks went very slightly pink.

'Would she do this with me?' he asked.

'Probably. I'll need to show you the commands. When you want her to circle, you do this.' She showed him the gesture and made him repeat it half a dozen times before she was satisfied. 'Good. She'll sit when you tell her. Then you need to get her to put her head on one side—she'll watch you and mirror you.' She talked him through the rest of the routine, then put the song on again and sat on the sofa, legs curled up, watching them as they went through the routine.

Luke knew his performance wasn't anywhere near as polished as Jess's had been, but even so he was blown away by the way the dog responded. He'd worked with animals before in his career, but it had never been like this. He'd never felt a real connection with the animals before. Not like it was with Baloo.

'You are just brilliant, Baloo.' He made a

fuss of the dog and looked up at Jess. 'Can I steal some of your treats for her?'

'Sure.' She fished the bag from her pocket and handed it to him, and Luke took great pleasure in feeding the dog some treats.

'Monica's going to be blown away by this, girl,' he said. He looked up at Jess. 'And it's all thanks to you.'

'Baloo's the one who did all the work,' she said.

'Coffee?' he asked. 'And we can watch the skyline light up.'

She nodded. 'I'd like that. That view's amazing.'

'Yeah.' Oddly, it pleased him that her thoughts were so in tune with his own.

They sat on the balcony with a mug of coffee until it was just too chilly to stay out, then came in to sit on the sofa. Baloo climbed up between them, settling herself with her nose on Jess's knee.

Jess went quiet on him again, but this time it was a different sort of quiet. The sort that made Luke think that she was silently gulping back the tears.

'Are you OK?' he asked.

She swallowed hard. 'Sure.'

But her tone was a little too bright. This was something to do with her ex and their dog, he was sure—the ones she didn't speak about. 'This is bringing back memories for you?' he guessed.

She nodded.

'Sorry.'

She took a deep breath and looked at him. 'Set rules?'

'Of course. Whatever you tell me stays with me.'

'Thank you.'

He frowned. 'What is it, Jess?'

She looked away. 'You know I was a trainer—well, it was with the police.'

'You were a policewoman?' Luke looked surprised. 'But I thought you said you did a degree in animal behaviour.'

'I did. But you have to do a couple of years on the beat before you can apply to train as a police dog handler,' she explained. 'When I joined the dog handling section, I stayed in touch with my old team. Being in the police—it's kind of like being in a family. You go through a lot together, so you're there for each other, even if you don't see each other every day.'

'A bit like working on a film set—you bond with the crew. Even the difficult ones.'

'I guess.'

'So you worked with sniffer dogs and that sort of thing?' he asked.

'Finding drugs? Yes, but that isn't the only work that the dogs do—they look for missing people, they work in search and rescue, and they track suspects.' Her throat closed when she thought about tracking suspects. That last job...

He waited in silence, and she knew he wasn't going to let her off the hook.

'I trained as a police dog handler. I did a few courses, and I was always involved when we did a display for the public at a show—the sort where you have a cops and robbers chase, and the dog takes the baddie down. Obviously the robber is one of the team and we use a protective sleeve so nobody gets hurt. I used to enjoy choreographing that.

'But it was only part of my job. I was shadowed by a trainee handler, and did some mentoring. That's when I found out how much I liked teaching. My boss asked me to consider training the handlers. I did some instructors' courses, and I loved it.' She shrugged. 'Obviously, if there was a big op, I could still help out as a handler. Most of the dogs are training to work with just their handler, but we also had dogs that were trained to work with several handlers.'

'I know I asked you before, and you said you didn't want to talk about it—but I really don't get why you gave up a job you loved to be a temp,' he said.

'Because…' She closed her eyes. The only way that she could get through telling him was if she could block everything else out. 'My husband was a handler, too. Your police dog lives with you until retirement, then generally becomes your pet. Comet was his. Mine, too, I guess, but Comet really adored Matt. He was a liver and white Springer Spaniel. We'd known him since the day he was born.' She blew out a breath. 'And it was Comet's last year in service. He was eight.'

Only eight. He'd still had years of life in him. His retirement years, when he could've been a much-loved family pet, happy to pad about the house or find himself a sunny spot in the garden where he could drowse the day away. And he hadn't had the chance.

'Matt was called out to a job. He'd had a tip from an informant about a drugs deal—he'd been trying to catch those particular dealers in the act for a while.' She dragged in a breath. 'But it was a set-up. They were lying in wait for him. They knew Matt would have a dog with him—the informant had fed back just as much information to the dealers as he'd given to the police, if not more.' And, because of that decision, her life had imploded.

'They targeted Comet first, put him out of action, then started beating Matt. Even though they broke his ribs and one of his legs, Comet still came after them and tried to protect Matt.' She swallowed hard. 'They shot him. They shot Matt, too. Then they left them both to die.' The words were getting harder and harder to say. She forced the tears back. 'They smashed Matt's phone so he couldn't call for help. He dragged himself into the street. God only knows how—he must have been in so much pain. But he wanted to try to save Comet. Someone found him and called an ambulance, and he told them as much as he could while they waited for the ambulance and the police to arrive—but he didn't make it to hospital. He died from massive blood loss on the way there.' Her throat felt raw with the effort of holding the tears back. 'Comet didn't make it, either.'

'God, Jess. I don't know what to say. But I'm so sorry you had to go through that.'

'I didn't even get the chance to say goodbye,' she whispered. 'I didn't get to say "I love you" one last time.'

'They knew,' he said fiercely. 'I'm sure they knew how much you loved them.'

Maybe. Except her last words to Matt had been… She squeezed her eyes even more tightly shut to block it out.

'When did it happen?' he asked softly.

'A year ago.' She'd gone completely to pieces afterwards. Especially after she lost the baby. Though she couldn't tell Luke about that.

Even so, to her surprise, words continued to pour out of her mouth, words that just refused to be held back now she'd started telling him about it.

'It's taken me a while to get my life back together. I managed to find a job with a temp agency. Doing pretty much anything and everything. I know it isn't what I was trained for, and I felt so guilty that I was wasting all that time and money and effort—but I needed to do a safe job. Something where nobody ever had a chance of getting hurt.'

'But you miss it, now?'

'I miss working with dogs, yes,' she admitted. 'I haven't been able to admit that there was this huge hole in my life, even to myself. My sister and my best friend have both nagged me about it.'

'Maybe you just needed time to work it out for yourself,' he said softly. 'I'm sorry. Looking after Baloo was the worst thing I could've asked you to do.'

'And the best.' She took a deep breath. 'Looking after her, training her—it's made me think, maybe I *can* go back. Not to the police. I can't handle the idea of training someone who's going to go out and get hurt, maybe killed. I just can't do it. But I could work with people like you. People who've just got their first dogs. Or maybe working with animals on film sets—all the risk assessments will be done to minimise the risk of an accident, and nobody's going to come in and hurt someone deliberately.' Her voice dropped to a raspy whisper. 'Nobody's going to *die*.'

Not only that, every job would have a different crew, Luke thought. Every job would have different animals. If she set up training classes for new owners, every course would have a different set of people. Which meant she wouldn't get involved, the way you would with a permanent set of colleagues. At heart, she was just like him, scared to get involved again.

Though she had much more reason to be scared. She'd lost everything through circumstances out of her control. He'd lost everything because he hadn't tried hard enough.

'I'm sorry you had to go through that,' he said again. 'And I get that I'm maybe asking you too much. If you know someone else who can help me…?'

'You don't want me to do it?'

'Not if it's going to be too hard for you. If it's going to rip everything open.'

'I'm always going to miss Matt and Comet. That'll never change. But they say that time heals. Every day it gets that tiny bit easier to handle.' She stroked Baloo's head. 'And Baloo here—I never expected that, but she's helped so much.'

'I'm glad,' he said softly, and reached over to squeeze her hand. And funny how it made his skin tingle all over. The lightest, gentlest contact. Crazy. It was almost like being a teenager again—that sense of expectation, of possibilities blooming, of everything being one step further into the exciting unknown.

Was it like this for her, too?

Not that he dared ask. Especially given what she'd just told him. And now he understood what she was struggling to get over: the death of the love of her life. His murder.

Maybe she wasn't ready for another relationship right now. Or maybe she felt the same pull that he did—despite not wanting to get involved, he found he couldn't help it.

Slowly. They needed to take this slowly. Not push too fast outside their comfort zones. And, right then, he just wanted to savour the moment and enjoy the kind of feeling he hadn't had for a very, very long time.

At the end of the evening, Luke insisted on driving Jess home, with Baloo in her crate in the back, and walked her to her front door. 'Goodnight, Jess,' he said. 'Have a good weekend.'

'You, too. Thank you for tonight.'

Her eyes were huge in the light from the street lamp, and he couldn't resist dipping his head to kiss her goodnight. He brushed his lips against hers. But once wasn't enough, and all his good intentions of taking it slowly just vanished as if they'd never been. He kissed her again. And again, until she kissed him back.

When he finally broke the kiss, they were both shaking.

'I'd better go. Baloo,' he said, gesturing to his car.

'Yeah.' Her voice sounded slightly rusty. Sexy as hell.

It almost made him yank her back into his arms. But his common sense prevailed.

Just.

'See you later,' he said, and fled back to the car, waiting until she'd closed the door behind her before driving away.

CHAPTER SIX

Is Luke lacking?

Luke caught his breath as he saw the headline on Saturday morning.

No. Surely not. Fleur wouldn't have told the press about *that*…would she?

Feeling sick, he read on.

Bad enough. The article was asking if he was lacking confidence, given that his last film was the first one for nearly ten years where he hadn't been nominated for a single award—would the new one be more of the same? The sly insinuation was that he'd passed his peak, this film was his last chance, and he was about to blow it.

He rolled his eyes. That was utterly ridiculous. Every actor or director made at least one film that didn't touch a chord with the audience as much as the others. You couldn't be at the top of the tree for your entire career. Life didn't work that way.

Was this story the handiwork of Fleur's cronies? Or maybe, he thought, Mimi's, given that he hadn't taken her up on her offers of being available. It could be her way of getting back at him, by hitting out at him professionally.

But he was just grateful that it wasn't the article he'd been dreading. The topic that Fleur had promised not to air—though that had been before the guilt kicked in and she'd started vilifying him to make herself feel better about the fact she'd cheated on him.

Is Luke lacking?

Yes.

Because he hadn't been able to give his wife the baby she wanted.

Some people coped with infertility. They had counselling, they tried IVF, they thought about different routes to having a family.

But Fleur hadn't wanted any of that. She'd just wanted a baby of her own, without having to go through invasive therapy or an emotional wringer. So she'd found herself someone who could provide what her husband couldn't.

Baloo wriggled her way onto his lap and licked his face.

He stroked her head. 'Are you trying to cheer me up?'

She wagged her tail hard.

'You're right. I should just stop the pity party and do something useful. Like take you for a walk.'

What had Jess said to him before?

A good run with a dog at your side will definitely put the world to rights. Even if you do have to go out in public wearing dark glasses and a silly hat.

'Do I need dark glasses and a silly hat?' he asked the dog.

Baloo just gave him that dopey doggy grin.

'Wearing dark glasses makes it look as if I've got something to hide.'

Well, he had. His infertility.

'Or as if I'm letting that article get to me— meaning there's some truth in it.'

Which there wasn't. Even though it had got to him, just a bit.

'Right, then. No hat,' he said. 'No glasses. We're going for a run, just as we are.'

He was surprised to discover that Jess was right. Going for a run with the dog by his side made him feel so much better and blew away some of the misery of that article. He had an endorphin rush from the run and he had the companionship of the dog. And other dog owners were smiling at him—not because he was Luke McKenzie, but because he had a dog with him and it was a shared fellowship.

When they got back to his house, Luke was feeling so much better. On impulse, he pulled out his mobile phone and typed a text to Jess. *You were right about taking the dog for a run.*

Then he paused. There was no point in sending this. She'd already said she was busy this weekend, and it wasn't fair to burden her with the way he felt. And sending that text would be pathetic and needy.

He could deal with this himself. Just like he had with every other emotional issue since his marriage imploded.

Grimacing, he pressed a button to delete the text.

You were right about taking the dog for a run.

Jess read the text and frowned.

Why would Luke send her such a cryptic message?

And what had she said to him about a run?

She racked her brain, then remembered. It was the evening when she'd teased him about his awful beanie hat. She'd told him that when you'd had a bad day, the best thing you could do was to go for a run with a dog at your side.

Which meant that Luke was having a

really bad day—particularly as he'd admitted that she was right.

They weren't shooting at the weekend, as far as she knew, so it couldn't be work. So was it his aunt? Had she taken a turn for the worse?

She called him. 'Hey, it's Jess,' she said when he answered.

'Jess?' He sounded shocked to hear from her.

'You just texted me,' she pointed out.

'No, I didn't.'

'So you haven't just taken Baloo for a run?'

'Ah. *That* text.' He sighed. 'I meant to delete that, not send it. My apologies.'

'Is everything OK?' she asked.

'Sure.'

'So your aunt's all right?' Jess persisted, convinced that something was wrong and he was bluffing. But he'd let her dump a load of stuff on him, last night. The least she could do would be to return the favour.

'Monica's a bit stir-crazy and dying to come home, but they're keeping an eye on her for a while longer yet.'

'That's good. I was worried that something might be wrong.'

'Why?'

She coughed. 'Let's try that again. If I'm

right about taking the dog for a run, it means you're having a bad day. So if it's not your aunt…'

He sighed. 'Ignore me. I just let a stupid article get to me, that's all.'

She knew she was probably speaking out of turn, but she couldn't help herself. 'It sounds as if you could do with tea and cake.'

'Tea and cake?' he asked.

'My sister's remedy for absolutely everything.'

'Does it work?'

And that sounded as if the words had come out before he could stop them. 'Usually.' She paused. 'If you have tea, I could bring some cake over.'

'I thought you were busy?'

Most of that had been an excuse so she didn't seem needy. Or like a stalker. 'I can always make time for cake.'

'Then thank you. Cake,' he said, 'sounds perfect.'

'See you in a bit.'

Jess went to the bakery round the corner from her flat to buy a selection of cakes, picked up some dog treats from the pet shop further down the parade of shops, and took the Tube to Luke's place. Remembering that kiss from last night made her feel slightly nervous about it. Was she doing the right thing? Was he going to think that her offer of comforting him with cake was going to be followed up by comforting him with kisses? And did she actually want to kiss him again?

The heat that flooded her skin told her that yes, she did.

Luke was the first man she'd been attracted to since Matt was killed. Part of Jess felt guilty about it—how could she want someone else, when it was only a year since she'd been widowed? And yet she knew that, had it been the other way round, she wouldn't have wanted Matt to spend the rest of his life pining for her.

And then again, how did Luke feel?

Not wanting to think too closely about that, she checked her phone to see if she could find the article that had thrown him off balance. She winced as she read it. How horrible to have people speculating about you in that way, and knocking your confidence. She was glad that she'd never had to deal with anything like that.

When she rang the doorbell, he opened the front door a few seconds later and the Labrador pushed her way in front of him, wriggling and wagging her tail wildly.

She grinned. 'Nice welcome, Baloo. And,

yes, I brought something for you.' She smiled at Luke. 'And for you.' She handed him the box.

He glanced inside when he'd ushered her indoors. 'These look wonderful—I don't believe this. Cupcakes with top hats on.'

'Well, with you being such a hat fiend...' she deadpanned.

He grinned. 'Yeah. Thank you. What tea would you like? Earl Grey? Rooibos and vanilla? Chai?'

Clearly he was a man after her own heart; she had a variety of teas in her own cupboard. 'Chai, please.'

'Chai it is.'

Luke had one of those posh glass teapots where you put loose-leaf tea in a basket in the centre that could be taken out when the tea was at the desired strength. And Jess noticed that he was careful not to put the tea into the water until they were both sitting on his balcony with a loaded tea tray in front of them. 'Tea, meet water. Water, meet tea,' he said, and pulled the centre out so he could pour her tea. 'This is basically stinky milk, you know,' he teased. 'All you're getting are the spices.'

'Just how I like it,' she said, and fed Baloo a dog treat while she waited for the tea to brew a bit more for him.

Sitting in the sunshine, overlooking the river, drinking tea and eating cupcakes: it was a perfect English summer afternoon. Apart from the fact that she wouldn't be here if Luke was happy. 'I read that article, by the way,' she said. 'I thought it was mean and underhand.'

He shrugged. 'I just have to let it roll.'

'Why can't you complain to the editor and make them apologise?'

'You know the saying, "Methinks the lady doth protest too much"?' he quoted. 'If I say something about it, then either I'm being stuck-up, or I'm trying to cover up the story. So it's better just to say nothing and not give it any more air.'

'It doesn't seem fair that people can say anything they like about you, and you have to shut up and take it.'

'Part and parcel of my job. Though it's not my favourite bit,' he admitted.

'I don't think any of your fans will agree with that article. They'll all say it's a load of tosh and your next film will be wonderful.'

'Strictly speaking,' he said, 'the last one *wasn't* my best film.'

He'd made it when he was in the middle of splitting up from Fleur, she guessed. So it was totally understandable. 'You can't be perfect all the time, and anyway your fans will forgive you a lot because of—well, what was happening in your life when you made it.'

'I try not to let my personal life get in the way of work,' he said, sounding slightly annoyed.

'I wasn't judging, Luke. Just saying that you're human.'

'Of course. Sorry.' He grimaced. 'I'm being oversensitive.'

'I guess it must knock your confidence when people give you a harsh review or come out with stuff like this.'

'That depends on how they do it. If they say what doesn't work for them and they're honest, then I can learn from it and make the next film better. I have no problem with that.'

'That's constructive criticism. Whereas this article…' She grimaced. 'It sounded to me more as if they had an axe to grind.'

'Maybe.' He looked uncomfortable, and she had the distinct impression that she was treading on a sore spot.

'So taking Baloo for a run helped?' she asked.

'Yes, it did,' he said. 'More than I expected.'

'Told you so. Strike two for Baloo,' she said.

'Jess,' he warned softly, 'I can't be her forever owner.'

'Methinks,' she said, throwing his words back at him, 'the lady—well, you're *not a lady, but you know what I mean*—doth protest too much. And I bet your aunt would say the same.'

'I'm just very glad you're not in the same room together,' he said wryly. 'You'd be a force to be reckoned with.'

'Now there's an idea,' she said lightly.

She finished her tea. 'I'd better be going—I'm expected at my sister's, and our parents are going to be there.' For a mad moment, she almost invited him to go with her; she knew Carly wouldn't mind Baloo turning up. But then why would an A-list actor want to hang out with a very ordinary family? 'I guess you'll be busy polishing your lines,' she said.

He gestured to the dog. 'And I have an audience to impress.'

'You'll impress your human audience, too,' she said softly. 'Don't let that article mess with your head. Go for another run with Baloo if you need to.' She paused. 'I'm probably speaking out of turn, here, but someone I know well had a really bad confidence wobble, a couple of years back. She went through a tough time at work. What got her through it was going to the gym and learning to lift weights.'

He raised an eyebrow. 'You're suggesting that's what I need to do? Go to a gym and lift weights?'

'For my friend, it was doing something totally different, something out of her comfort zone. The discipline of training helped her focus and it helped her to get her confidence back.' She looked at him. 'You've hit a tough patch. The discipline of training Baloo might do the same thing for you that the gym did for her—it's out of your comfort zone, but seeing the dog's progress and knowing that you're the one responsible for it...' She wrinkled her nose and shook her head. 'Oh, I'll shut up. I've already said too much.'

'You were right about the running. Maybe you're right about this.' He paused. 'Jess, thanks. I really appreciate you being there for me.'

'Hey. That's what friends are for.' She shrugged off his praise, but secretly it warmed her. 'Thanks for the tea. See you Monday.'

'Thanks for the cake. See you Monday.'

And, when Luke ushered her downstairs, it felt only natural for Jess to pause by the front door. To look at him. He was looking right back at her, his pupils wide and his eyes an incredible silver-grey. Almost in slow motion, his hand came up to cup her face. He rubbed his thumb gently along her lower lip. 'Jess,' he said softly, and she knew he was going to kiss her again. She couldn't help tipping her head back slightly in offering. Softly, gently, he brushed his lips against hers, and that breezy goodbye on his balcony was completely undermined. She opened her mouth, letting him deepen the kiss, and somehow his arms were wrapped tightly round her and her hands were tangled in his hair.

When he broke the kiss, they were both shaking. His gaze held hers and for a moment she thought he was going to ask her to stay. But then he stroked her face again. 'Sorry. I seem to be making a habit of this.'

Jess wasn't sorry in the slightest. 'So you do.' She reached up to touch her mouth to his. 'See you Monday,' she whispered.

He stole another kiss. 'Monday.'

And Jess had the distinct feeling that next Monday wouldn't come fast enough for either of them.

On Sunday, Luke divided his time between training Baloo with the exercises Jess had already taught him, and working on polishing his lines.

But, despite what he'd told Jess the previous day about never letting his personal life distract him, he found himself getting very distracted indeed. Especially when he thought about how Jess had kissed him back yesterday.

This was insane. They both had baggage, valid reasons for not getting involved with someone else. And yet she was so unlike the showbiz women he was used to mixing with; she was utterly straightforward. And she made him laugh. She could tease him out of a dark mood—and comfort him with kisses.

But what could he offer her, beyond a lifestyle? He had no idea whether she wanted children—they were nowhere near the stage of their relationship where they could discuss that—but his infertility could turn out to be a deal-breaker, just like it had with Fleur. Did he really want to let himself fall all the way in love with her, only to have to let her walk away?

As if sensing his mood, Baloo put her paws on his knees and licked his nose.

'You, too,' he said. 'I can't offer you a proper future. And it's mean to let you bond with me. And stupid of me to get used to having you around.' Though one thing had become very clear over the last week—having the dog around had really made his house feel like home, instead of just a place to live.

Maybe there was some way he could find a compromise.

Maybe.

When Luke walked on to the set on Monday, he quickly discovered that everyone was pussyfooting round him; he sighed inwardly, knowing they'd read the article. How many of them agreed with it? he wondered.

The only one who didn't handle him with kid gloves was Jess. She tapped her watch and rolled her eyes, really hamming it up. 'What time do you call this? Talk about messing with a poor, hard done by Labrador's routine. Off to work with you, McKenzie. Baloo here needs a nap.'

He could've hugged her for that. Because the teasing, and the way Jess didn't look at him as if he was so fragile that one word out of place would make him shatter, made all the tension flood out of his muscles. She believed in him.

'My apologies, O Great Animal Expert.' He made a fuss of Baloo. 'See you after shooting. Don't steal or chew anything except a dog toy, OK?'

'As if she would,' Jess teased. 'Break a leg.'

'Thanks.' He blew a kiss at Ayesha. 'See you guys later.'

During filming, he found the rest of the crew were still treating him with kid gloves. When they took a break at the end of the first scene, he said, 'Can I have a quick cast conference, here?'

George, the director, looked surprised. 'What's up?'

'Very, *very* quick cast conference,' Luke said.

George called everyone to gather round.

'I'm guessing you all saw that article at the weekend,' Luke said. 'Guys, you don't have to treat me like a special snowflake. OK, so I didn't get nominated for an award for my last film. So what? It's just one film, and it's not the same as this one. Just so you all know, whatever that article said, this is going to be a great movie. The script is great, we're all doing our jobs to the best of our ability, and our audiences are going to laugh and cry in all the places we want them to. We're a team. And I'm not intending to let any of you down, OK?'

'OK. That's good enough for me.' George clapped his shoulder. 'And I'll talk to the publicity team and see if they can fix up some interviews to show that you're doing just fine.'

The rest of the cast from the scene followed suit, shaking his hand and agreeing with him. Except, he noticed, Mimi. So maybe she'd been the one feeding the information to the journalist. Revenge for turning her down? Or maybe it was because she'd been friendly with Fleur at some point. He didn't know and he didn't care. But he wasn't going to give her any chance to try that kind of stunt again.

CHAPTER SEVEN

ON FRIDAY JESS was taking Baloo for a walk in the park when she felt a tug on her shoulder; acting purely on instinct, she grabbed the top of her bag and looked round. A young lad in a hoodie was tugging on the strap of her bag.

He honestly thought she was just going to let him mug her, in broad daylight, in the middle of the park? 'Get off!' she yelled, expecting him to drop the strap of her bag and run off.

To her shock, he produced a knife. 'Give me your bag,' he demanded.

Her stomach turned to water. So he wasn't just an opportunist thief who could be scared off by attention being drawn to him, then. And, from the slurred sound of his voice, he was taking some kind of drug that clearly made him feel invincible. He'd have no hesitation in sticking that knife straight into her.

Give him the bag.

That would be the sensible thing to do.

But the bag had her phone in it. With photos of Matt and Comet. Texts from Matt that she hadn't been able to bear to delete.

She couldn't lose them. *Especially not today.*

'I said, give me the bag,' he snarled again.

Baloo barked, then growled at him; he turned on the dog and kicked her hard in the ribs. Baloo yelped and hit the ground.

And then Jess's police training kicked in. Everything went into slow motion, as if she were wading through treacle. The next thing she knew, the mugger was on the floor with his arm twisted between his shoulder blades, the knife was safely out of his reach, and her knee was pressed into the small of his back.

'You'd better hope my dog's all right,' she snarled. 'If you've hurt her…'

It would be oh, so easy to pull his arm that little bit tighter and snap the bone. To hurt him as he'd hurt her dog. To grab his hair and keep smacking his head into the ground. To hurt him in revenge for all the thugs like him who hurt people—thugs like the ones who'd beaten Comet and left Matt to bleed to death.

So, so easy.

And so, so wrong.

'Someone call the police,' she yelled. She glanced over at Baloo, who was sitting beside her, shaking.

'It's all right, sweetheart,' she soothed. Please let Baloo be all right. Please don't let the thug have broken her ribs or caused internal bleeding.

Again, she had to resist the urge to grind the mugger's face into the dirt and snap a bone or two.

People crowded round her. She was aware of people offering to help, to take over from her, but she wasn't letting the mugger go or risk the chance of him escaping. She wanted him cuffed and charged. And she wanted him stopped in this way of life, before he really hurt someone.

'Is this his?' one of the bystanders asked, bending towards the knife.

'Yes. Don't touch it,' Jess warned. 'It's evidence and we don't want his fingerprints compromised.'

'What, you're a pig?' the mugger asked with a last bit of drug-induced bravado, using the derogatory nickname for the police.

Not any more, she wasn't, but he didn't need to know that. But she had no intention of engaging in conversation with him. Not until his rights had been read to him, and she couldn't do that herself any more.

At last, she heard the familiar wail of a police siren.

Two police officers came rushing over. 'What's going on here? Oh, Jess!' one of them said in surprise.

She recognised the two officers as colleagues from her old station.

'Mikey, Ray,' she acknowledged them both. 'This guy tried to mug me and grab my bag. He pulled a knife on me—' she nodded to indicate the weapon that he'd dropped earlier '—and he kicked my dog. I'm happy to testify in court, and I want you to make sure animal cruelty is added to the rap sheet.'

'You hurt my arm,' the mugger whined. 'And your dog tried to bite me.'

Jess raised her eyebrows. 'I think you'll find that I've used appropriate force, and no more. And my dog didn't try to bite you. You were threatening me with a knife and she growled at you. You *kicked* her, you bastard.' She felt her muscles go tight. Right at that moment, she wanted to kick the mugger. Where it hurt. Really, really hard.

'OK. We'll take it from here. And we need to take a proper statement from you, Jess,' Mikey said.

She relinquished her hold on the thug. While the officers read the mugger his rights and cuffed him, she checked Baloo, gently feeling the area where the dog had been kicked.

Baloo whined, but Jess hoped that it was because the dog was scared and sore, rather than because she had broken ribs. She couldn't feel anything like a break. But the bastard had kicked her hard. Jess thought again about what had happened to Comet; she only just managed to hold it together, aware that she was shaking now as much as the dog was.

'Are you OK to give a statement here, Jess? Do you need someone to get you a mug of hot sweet tea or something?' Ray asked.

'I'm fine,' Jess said, as if saying it would make it true, and sat on the floor so Baloo could creep onto her lap. So what if a Labrador was way too big to be a lapdog? Right now the dog needed comfort—and so did Jess.

She gave a clear description of exactly what had happened, all the while soothing the dog and holding her close.

'And you'll testify in court, if we need you to?' Ray checked.

'Absolutely.'

'Great. Well, we'll be in touch and let you know what happens.'

She got to her feet again to sign the statement, and he hugged her. 'It's good to see you again. We've all missed you, you know.'

'I missed you all, too. But, after what happened…'

'Yeah, we know. It's…' Ray blew out a breath. 'It's hard.'

He could actually have a lunch break today? Delighted with the news, Luke rang Jess to see if she was free for lunch. No answer. Well, she was probably busy at the production office. He called in to see her, only to discover from Ayesha that Jess had already taken Baloo to the park. Well, OK—it wasn't that huge a park. He'd probably be able to spot them within a couple of minutes.

He signed out of the set and crossed over to the park. He could see a police car parked across the road with blue lights flashing, and there appeared to be a crowd of people in the park. He glanced over briefly, and then stood absolutely still with shock.

Jess was right in the middle of that crowd. With Baloo. And the police were talking to her.

What the…?

Forcing himself to stay calm, he walked over to join her. 'Hey, Jess. Is everything OK?' Stupid question. Of course it wasn't.

'It's fine now,' she said. 'Nothing to worry about.'

But her voice was slightly brittle, and he knew she was keeping something back. Something important.

'You take care, Jessie. And call us. We'd all like to see you,' one of the policemen said, hugging her.

'I will, Mikey.'

'Promise?'

She smiled and patted his shoulder. 'Promise.'

What was going on?

He guessed that maybe Jess had worked with the policemen or their partners in the past, but something was very clearly wrong.

'Are you all right?' he asked again.

'I'm fine.'

He didn't think she was. There was no colour whatsoever in her face and her eyes were huge. 'What's happened, Jess?'

She took a deep breath. 'We were mugged. A guy tried to grab my bag. He had a knife.'

Luke went cold. This could've been much, much worse. Jess could've been seriously hurt. 'Oh, my God.'

She flapped a dismissive hand. 'I disarmed him and it's OK now. He's in custody.'

'You need some hot sweet tea,' he said. 'And some space.' People were crowding round, still. And he didn't think it was just the mugging that had attracted them; people were beginning to nudge each other and point at him, too. 'Let's go back to the set. Find somewhere quiet so you can sit down and catch your breath.' He shepherded her and Baloo out of the park. He'd also noticed that the dog hadn't leapt all over him, the way she usually did; instead, Baloo was subdued and clinging to Jess's side. Clearly the mugging had frightened the dog badly.

He got them both signed back into the set, then bought them both a drink and a sandwich at the catering tent before taking her back to his trailer.

'Thank you,' she said softly, clearly on the edge of tears. He was shocked by how protective it made him feel. He wanted to wrap her up and keep her safe. And he wanted to pin that mugger against the wall and put the fear of God into him so the kid never, ever tried to hurt someone again.

He blew out a breath and unclenched his fists.

'It's hot and sweet. I thought it might help,'

he said, pushing the paper cup of tea towards her. 'And, if you want to talk, I'm here.'

Oh, God. He was being so nice, Jess thought. And she was just a mess.

He'd meant well, she knew. Hot sweet tea was supposed to be good for shock. But even the scent of it made her gag, bringing back memories of the last time someone had made her hot sweet tea. Gallons of the stuff, while the bad news unfolded and unfolded and unfolded until it swamped her.

She swallowed hard. 'I'm sorry. I can't drink it.'

He rummaged in the fridge. 'I have sparkling water or milk, or I can make you some instant coffee.'

She shook her head. 'Thanks, but I don't want anything.' Her throat felt swollen from holding back the tears. Right at that moment, she didn't think she could swallow food or drink.

Luke gave her space while she toyed with the sandwich he'd bought her and fed all the chicken to Baloo.

'I have cyber cake,' he said, taking his phone out of his pocket and finding a picture of cake on the internet. 'Not *quite* as good as your sister's remedy, but it'll have to do at short notice.'

She gave him a watery smile. 'Thanks for trying.'

'Talk to me, Jess,' he said softly. 'Better out than in. And it's set rules. It won't go further than me.'

She dragged in a breath. 'I guess today brought a lot of things back to me.' Her voice was shaky. 'The mugger kicked Baloo. I wanted to break his arm and get revenge for Matt and Comet. I really wanted to hurt him, Luke. That's exactly why I can't be a police dog trainer any more. I can't send handlers and dogs into difficult situations where some bastard could put a bullet through them and leave them to die, the way it happened to Matt and Comet. And I can't trust myself to be a good cop and act according to the law.'

'But you didn't hurt the guy,' he reminded her. 'You disarmed him and you got someone to call the police.'

'But I *wanted* to hurt him, and that's the point—what if I'd lost control?'

'I don't think you would,' he said.

'I can't take that risk. It wouldn't be fair on anyone. I'd be a liability to work with.' She shook her head. 'That's why I resigned. I can't go back to the force. Ever.' And for all this to be brought back to her today, of all days…

She was crying silently, tears sliding down her face. The dog was anxious, nudging Jess with her nose and whining.

Luke put his arms round both of them, holding them close. 'Jess. You don't have to go back. You don't have to do anything you don't want to.' He kissed the top of her head. 'It's OK. I'm here. So's Baloo.'

And that made her feel even more guilty. This attraction she felt towards Luke—how much of it was for his sake, and how much was her trying to replace Matt and Comet?

'I'm sorry.' Jess scrubbed at her eyes with the back of her hand. 'I was being wet.'

'Don't be so hard on yourself,' Luke said softly, knowing he was being a hypocrite because he'd done exactly the same thing when his marriage broke up.

She ignored his comment. 'I need to get Baloo to the vet's. I checked her over myself and I'm pretty sure she's just bruised and frightened and shocked, but I want to be double sure that she doesn't have any broken bones.'

Or internal bleeding, he thought—this had clearly brought back everything that had happened to Comet. Hadn't she said that the thugs had broken the dog's ribs and a leg?

'I'll come with you.'

She shook her head. 'You can't. You're expected back on set.' She bit her lip. 'And I've probably already ruined the continuity and what have you—I've made wet patches on your shirt.'

'Wardrobe can sort that out later. This is a question of priorities.'

'Luke, people are depending on you. Baloo will be safe with me.' She gave a mirthless laugh. 'Well, she should have been safe with me in the park, but she wasn't, was she?'

'It isn't your fault.'

'Yes, it is. If the mugger hadn't targeted me she'd be fine.'

'Does it not occur to you,' he pointed out gently, 'that it's actually the mugger's fault? He was the one who chose to try and steal your bag. He could see that you had a dog with you and everyone knows how loyal dogs are. He must've known that the dog would bark or growl at him.'

She dragged in a breath. 'Even so. Look, I'll text you from the vet's. Keep your phone on silent.'

Luke realised that this was her way of saying she wanted some space. Right now she probably wanted to get her equilibrium back. Half of it was the shock of being mugged and half of it was from the memories it had brought back.

So he needed to back off. Now. 'OK. I'll wait to hear from you.'

'And this time,' she said, 'I promise I'll keep your dog safe.'

He didn't have the heart to remind her that Baloo was only his dog temporarily. 'I know. I trust you.'

But the look on her face said it all. She didn't trust herself.

Yeah. He knew what that felt like, too.

Jess texted Luke from the vet's. *All fine. Just bruising. No scary stuff.*

She was surprised to get a text back immediately. *Good. Stop worrying. See you both later.*

Maybe he was on a break between scenes. He wouldn't have ruined a scene just for her, would he?

'Well, *we* are going back to the park on the way to the set,' she told Baloo. 'We're going to face it now, so it doesn't get a chance to scare us and get blown out of proportion.'

The dog just looked trustingly at her.

It was enough to break her heart all over

again. Remembering how Comet had looked trustingly at her and Matt. They hadn't been able to keep Comet safe. Matt hadn't been able to keep himself safe, either.

She dragged in a breath. 'Is it ever going to stop hurting, Baloo? Am I ever going to be able to move on?'

The dog licked her.

'I want to, I really do. And I think I want to move on with Luke.' She enjoyed his company. He made her world feel brighter. 'But what if that goes wrong? What if someone hurts him? There are some seriously crazy people out there, people who'll try to hurt others to get their two minutes or whatever of fame.' She sighed. 'I'm a mess. I'm not ready for this. Maybe I need to start backing off.'

Baloo whined.

'Come on. Time for the park. No stupid muggers are going to scare us off,' she said, straightening her shoulders, and set off with the dog.

Luke walked into the production office as usual after shooting had finished for the day.

'Come and have dinner with us?' he asked.

She wanted to say yes, she really did. But the look of sympathy on his face made the tears prick at the back of her eyelids again.

Supposing they went out and she ended up sobbing all over him again? She couldn't face it. It had been bad enough having a meltdown in his trailer. 'Please don't think I'm being rude,' she said carefully, 'and it's really nice of you to ask, but I don't think I can face going out tonight.'

He shrugged. 'OK. We'll go back to mine and I'll cook for you.'

She shook her head. 'That's really kind of you, but no.'

'You've had a horrible day,' he said softly. 'It's brought back a lot of bad memories for you and, although you might think you want to be alone, I think you really need some company.'

Why did he have to be so nice? So understanding? Why couldn't he be the archetypal arrogant millionaire type, the sort who never gave a second thought to anyone else and their needs—the sort she'd want to push into a puddle? Someone as inconsiderate and mean as Luke's leading lady in the film? Someone she could despise instead of want to be with?

She didn't trust herself to answer and just stared mutely at him.

'If you don't want to go to my place, we'll go to yours—and I'll cook.'

Help. The idea of Luke McKenzie in her tiny galley kitchen, working with her in such intimate surroundings... 'You don't have to cook for me. Besides, I haven't been shopping this week and my fridge is pretty empty.' Way to go, Jess. Couldn't you have come up with a more feeble excuse? she berated herself.

'Then we'll get a pizza delivered,' he said.

She panicked. 'I'm not supposed to have dogs.'

'If your landlord complains, I'll explain that it's my fault and charm him out of giving you any hassle.' He smiled at her. 'Being charming is part of my job description, remember.'

She knew he was right. Although part of her wanted to be alone, left to her own devices she would just curl into a ball and sob herself to sleep. She probably did need company.

'OK,' she said, knowing she was beaten. 'Thank you.' And she followed him and Baloo to his car.

CHAPTER EIGHT

WHEN LUKE PARKED in the street outside Jess's house, she climbed out of the car. 'Bring Baloo in and I'll get you a parking permit.'

She unlocked the front door, very aware of how dark and cramped her flat would seem to him after his light, spacious townhouse, and walked through to the kitchen. She grabbed the parking permit pad from the drawer and swiftly scribbled out the details.

Luke and Baloo came into the kitchen just as she'd finished.

'You just need to add your car registration number,' she said, handing Luke the permit and a pen.

He filled in the last bit, and Baloo whined and barked as he left to put the permit in his car.

Jess dropped to her knees and put her arms round the dog's neck. 'Shh, sweetheart. If next door hears you, then we'll be toast. He'll tell the landlord.'

Baloo whined and licked her cheek.

She made a fuss of the dog and then put the kettle on.

When Luke came back into the kitchen, she didn't look round. 'Sorry, I don't have a posh coffee-making machine like yours, but I do have decent coffee.' She took the jar of ground coffee from the fridge and shook some into a cafetière.

Jess was really nervous, Luke thought, but he had absolutely no idea why. Did she think he'd look down on her because she didn't have a posh flat with a river view?

'So can you recommend a pizza delivery place?' he asked.

'I guess.' She rummaged in a drawer and took out a flyer. 'I normally get a thin crust.'

'Fine by me. Margherita?'

'Whatever.'

She sounded so tired, so hurt. He wanted to hold her close and tell her that he'd never let anything bad happen to her again. But it was a promise he couldn't keep. Life had a nasty habit of throwing curveballs. Besides, he didn't want to spook her. There was a fine line between being supportive and smothering her.

He called the pizza place to order dinner.

'Would you like some wine?' she asked when he put the phone down again.

'I'm driving, so better stick to something soft—but don't let that stop you.'

She shook her head. 'I'm fine. I'm not going to bother.'

Luke noticed how plain everything was. How bare the kitchen surfaces were. Given how close she'd seemed to her sister and best friend, he'd expected to see photographs of them all together, held to the fridge with magnets—but there was nothing. This didn't feel like a home, and it certainly didn't feel as if it belonged to the Jess he'd come to know. The flat felt as anonymous as a hotel suite, just a place to live.

She ushered him through to the living room; he sat on the small sofa, and Baloo settled herself on the floor by his feet. There was a small bistro table like the one on his balcony, with two chairs. There were a couple of prints on the walls that Luke guessed had come with the furnished flat, because they were as bland and anonymous as the decor. There were no photographs or any kind of ornament on the fireplace—no pictures of her husband or her family or the dog.

It was as if Jess had just shut everything away.

The pizza, when it finally arrived, was really indifferent. Not that Luke cared. He was more worried about Jess. She'd closed off on him.

'Shall I make us some more coffee?' he asked.

She shrugged, as if it was too much effort to disagree.

He couldn't leave her like this. He walked over to her, scooped her out of her chair, and sat down in her place, settling her onto his lap and holding her close. 'Jess, talk to me.'

She just looked at him, her green eyes huge and her face chalk-white again.

'It's better out than in,' he said, knowing himself to be a total hypocrite because he never talked about the real reason he and Fleur had broken up. How often those same words had been said to him, too. *Better out than in*. He wouldn't know.

A tear slid slowly down her cheek. 'It's an anniversary.'

Anniversary? he thought. It couldn't be the murder. She'd said it was over a year ago since she'd lost Matt and Comet.

'I was pregnant when Matt died.'

Luke went cold. The one topic that he never wanted to talk about. Pregnancy.

But if he stopped her talking now, he'd have to explain. He didn't want to do that. He didn't want Jess to know how much of a failure he was.

She dragged in a breath. 'I had a fight with Matt, the morning of the day he was killed. I can't even remember what it was about. Something trivial. I felt sick all morning, and then it hit me that my period was late. I bought a test. It was positive. So I thought maybe that's why I'd been so touchy and we'd had that fight—it was all just stupid hormones. I should've called him and told him right there and then, but I wanted to wait until he got home. I wanted to tell him face to face, and say sorry.'

Except she hadn't had the chance, Luke thought, so Matt had never known that he was going to be a father.

Luke knew he ought to say something but he didn't know what to say. He didn't know how to comfort her. Just as he'd failed to comfort his wife and failed to give her the baby she'd wanted so much.

Not wanting Jess to see his face and guess

that something was wrong, he enfolded her in another hug. 'The anniversary?' he prompted.

'I lost the baby.' She dragged in a breath. 'I know miscarriages are really common in early pregnancy, but even so it was the last straw for me. I wanted that baby so much.'

Just like Fleur. Jess had wanted a baby with Matt. If Luke let her get any closer to him, maybe she'd start wanting a baby with him, too. The one thing he couldn't give her.

'I thought I still had something left of him. When I lost the baby, I lost the last link to him. And I felt so guilty.'

'Oh, honey. I don't know what to say.'

And he didn't know how to stop her hurting. How to stop himself hurting. Though wild horses wouldn't drag that information from him.

How different his life might have been if he hadn't had mumps when he was ten. He could've had a son. A daughter. Maybe one of each.

Then again, he wouldn't have met Jess. He wouldn't have been here with her right now, holding her. So maybe things happened for a reason.

'It wasn't your fault.' He kissed her gently. 'Jess. Is that why you don't have any photos up?'

'Because I feel guilty and I can't face it?' She rested her forehead against his. 'Yes.'

'Do you still have photos?'

'They're packed away.'

'You need to look at them, Jess, not shut them out of your life. They're part of who you are.'

She looked at him, her face full of misery.

'Show me,' he said softly.

He thought she was going to refuse. Then she nodded, slid off his lap and left the room. She was gone for so long that he was at the point of going to look for her; but then she walked in with a large box.

There were framed pictures on the top. She handed him the first one in silence.

Clearly she'd married Matt when they were both in their very early twenties; they both looked young and fresh-faced. Matt looked like a decent guy; and in the photograph his face was full of love.

'You were a beautiful bride,' Luke said softly. 'You look so happy together. Anyone can see how you really loved each other.' He stroked her hair back from her face. 'Hold on to that, Jess. There was always the love there.'

Though in a way he knew he was a hypocrite. He couldn't stand to look at his own wedding photographs, because he was scared

he'd see traces of Fleur's faithlessness in them
even then.

More framed photographs: her graduation, and Matt's. A picture of a woman in a
wedding dress and Jess in what was clearly a
bridesmaid's dress; they resembled each other
enough for him to guess that the bride was
Jess's sister Carly. A second wedding picture,
again with Jess in what looked like a bridesmaid's dress, smiling broadly with a bride.
'Is that Shannon?' he asked.

She nodded. 'My best friend.'

Group pictures—Jess and what he assumed
were her family in a garden, with a dog smack
in the middle of the group that just had to be
Comet. Jess cuddling babies; those pictures
made his stomach knot, but he wasn't going
to let her know how much it affected him.
This was about her, not the mess of his life.
It was about her taking control and taking her
life back. And he wanted to help her do that.
Lend her some of his strength.

After the framed pictures, there were al-
bums. Jess's wedding. An album of family
pictures—weddings, christenings, candid
shots at Christmas and on summer after-
noons. Pictures of a tiny spaniel puppy with
a snub nose and floppy ears; more pictures
of the dog as he grew up and filled out, his

ears and nose growing longer, feathery hair appearing on his legs. Pictures of Matt in uniform with the dog. Another picture that looked as if it commemorated some kind of bravery award.

'Comet,' she whispered.

As if hearing the distress in Jess's voice, Baloo came over to put her chin on Jess's knee.

The tiny gesture was the one to make Jess crack again, and she cried all over Luke and Baloo.

He held her until her sobs died down, and Baloo licked Jess's face anxiously.

'I'm sorry,' she whispered eventually.

'Don't apologise. It's fine.'

'I've given you such a rubbish evening.'

'Actually, you haven't. You've given me trust, and you've told me things you haven't told anyone else. That's worth a lot.' He paused. 'Jess. Do you want me to stay?'

'You can't. Baloo,' she said.

'Then come and stay at mine. You can't be alone tonight.'

She shook her head. 'Right now, I think I need some space. But I appreciate the offer.' She stroked his face. 'Thank you. You've been utterly brilliant.'

'I'm just glad I could be there for you,'

Luke said, and was shocked to realise how much he meant that. It wasn't just a kind platitude—he really was glad that he'd made Jess talk to him and open her heart.

Just as long as she didn't expect him to do the same. Because he just couldn't admit to how much of a failure he really was.

'Do you want me to call anyone for you? Carly? Shannon?'

She shook her head. 'I'll be OK. Really. I think I just need a bath and an early night. But thank you for being here.' She hugged him. 'I'll call you tomorrow.'

'OK. If you change your mind, just call me. I'll come and get you.'

'Thank you.'

Maybe he was pushing her now, but he didn't want her to go back into her shell, the way he suspected she'd done after Matt and Comet were killed and she'd lost the baby. 'Are we still on for tomorrow?' he asked.

'Tomorrow?' She looked dazed. 'What about tomorrow?'

'Last weekend, you said you'd cook for me and we'd take Baloo out on the Thames Path.'

For a moment, he thought she was going to back out, but then she gave him a weary smile. 'I swear you're channelling my sister.'

'I am. Nagging's good. And I'll buy cake.'

'You'll leave Baloo on her own in your house, for long enough to go to the shop and buy cake?' she asked.

'Well, someone gave me some very good advice about a toy stuffed with treats. Which will distract her for long enough for me to buy not just cake, but *awesome* cake.' He kissed her very lightly. 'Say yes.'

She dragged in a breath. 'Yes. And I promise not to cry all over you tomorrow.'

'Deal,' he said. What he really wanted to do was to carry her to his car, take her back to his place and just hold her until she slept, but he knew she needed some space. 'Mañana,' he said, kissing her one last time.

When he'd gone, Jess headed to the bathroom, leaving the box of photographs where it was. She couldn't face putting them all away again. Not right now.

The bath didn't help much. She cleaned the kitchen, then dragged herself to bed, and finally fell asleep with tears seeping down her cheeks again.

CHAPTER NINE

JESS WOKE EARLY on Saturday morning with a thumping headache from all the crying the night before. She splashed her face with water and took some paracetamol, then looked at the photographs she'd left in the living room. Did she really want to box her past up like that and shut it away? She remembered what Luke had said. *They're part of who you are.* She knew he was right. Slowly, she picked up the photo frames and put them on the mantelpiece one by one. Comet. Matt. Their wedding day. Graduation. Her sister's wedding. Shannon's wedding.

So much love.

She wouldn't shut it out any more.

After a shower and washing her hair, she went out to buy flowers, then headed for the cemetery where Matt and Comet were buried. The last of the early summer bulbs had finished flowering, and she made a mental note to bring secateurs next time to tidy up the plot.

She put the flowers in the vase in front of the headstone. 'Hey, Matt. I've put the photos back up.' It still hurt to look at the pictures, a reminder of what she'd lost, but she was trying to see it the other way. That they were part of who she was.

'I'm not putting you out of my heart, but I've spent the last year living in the shadows with everything on hold. And maybe, just maybe, it's time to take my life back.' She swallowed hard. 'I always thought we'd grow old together and raise children. You would've made such a great dad.' Tears threatened to break up her words again. 'And I'm so sorry I couldn't carry our baby to term. So sorry that I couldn't give your parents another generation to love.' She paused. 'If I'd been the one who was killed, then I would've wanted you to meet someone else.' Though she still felt guilty that she was the one left behind. The one who'd met someone else.

She sighed. 'I've kind of met someone else. Though he's way out of my league. As if an international film star's really going to be interested in an ordinary woman like me. But he's had a hard time, too. He's lost someone he loved. So maybe this is a fling, the thing that gets his life and my life back on track. Something to make us both live again.' She rearranged the flowers. 'I'll always love you, Matt. You'll always be part of me, you and Comet. I just—I just wish it hadn't been this way. And I hope you understand.'

There was a soft hiss of wind through the branches of the trees, almost as if someone was whispering the word 'yes'.

Or maybe she was just being way too fanciful.

All the same, Jess went home feeling better. As if someone had taken down a blackout blind from a window and the sun was shining into the room.

Maybe today was the day her life started over.

She'd promised Luke dinner. It didn't take long to get the ingredients at the supermarket. And she found herself humming along to the radio as she cooked. How long had it been since her heart had felt this light? And she was pretty sure that it was all down to Luke and Baloo.

She put the finished dish in an airtight container so it wouldn't leak in her bag on the way to Luke's, put the rest of the ingredients and a bottle of wine in another bag, and took the Jubilee Line out to Bermondsey.

It was a ten-minute walk from the Tube station to Luke's house. With every step she took, Jess was more and more aware of the adrenaline racing through her bloodstream. By the time she reached his front door and rang the bell, her heart felt as if it were drumming so loudly the whole world must be able to hear it.

Luke opened the door, wearing faded jeans and a white shirt, looking utterly gorgeous. Jess was sure that her face had gone hot and red, betraying her feelings. Please don't let him have any idea about how star-struck she'd become, she begged silently.

Baloo was pattering round his feet and wagged her tail madly; Jess was glad of the excuse to bend down and make a fuss of her.

'Hello, there.' Luke smiled at her.

What she was going to say went straight out of her head. In the end, she gabbled, 'One green Thai chicken curry—I made it this morning so it'll have time for the flavours to mature in the fridge while we're out.' She handed him the bag with the tub of curry. 'I'll make the rice and steamed veg when we get back.' She handed him another bag.

'What's this?' he asked.

'Jasmine rice, coriander, cashews, a lime and some tenderstem broccoli—oh, and a bottle of wine.' Oh, for pity's sake, Jess—how to sound like a gibbering idiot. Stop *talking*, she commanded herself.

He peered into the bag. 'Chablis. How fabulous.'

'It's nice and crisp, so it will go well with a curry.' Matt had always been the wine buff; Jess had just picked up the knowledge from him over the years.

'Thank you. Come up for a minute while I put this in the fridge and sort out Baloo's stuff.'

She followed Luke into the kitchen and waited while he put everything away. Then he took Baloo's leash from a drawer and clipped it onto her collar. 'I've got her bowl, a bottle of water and a supply of plastic bags,' he said, taking a bag from the worktop, 'so I think we're ready. I'm looking forward to playing tour guide.' He smiled at her. 'We've got a nice day for it. I thought we could stop off somewhere and have an ice cream overlooking the river.'

'That sounds lovely.' And please, please, please let her common sense kick in soon. Please let her stop wanting him to hold her hand and kiss her. Please.

'No dark glasses or silly hats?' she asked.

He grinned and produced a fez. 'I was thinking of wearing this one.' His grin broadened. 'Especially for you.'

She couldn't help laughing, every bit of nervousness dispelled. 'No chance. Glasses I'll allow, as it's sunny. But no hat.'

'Spoilsport,' he grumbled, but his eyes were sparkling with amusement.

'Ready to go walkies?' he asked the dog, who woofed and wagged her tail.

When he'd locked the front door, they headed for the riverside path. They stopped by a low tumbledown brick wall at the edge of an uneven green space. 'This was the manor house of Edward III. Most of the ruins are buried under the green behind that wall,' Luke said. 'Just over there's the park named after the stairs that used to lead to the manor—the mudlarks used it, too.'

'Mudlarks?' Jess asked.

'Children who used to scavenge in the river mud for treasures,' he explained. 'This used to be quite a poor area.'

They followed the path along the riverbank. Jess noticed a couple of women nudging each other and looking at Luke. Then one of them came over. 'Excuse me—Mr McKenzie?' she asked.

He smiled at her. 'Luke.'

She went pink. 'Would you, um, mind having a picture taken with me, please?'

'Sure,' he said easily. 'What's your name?'

'Diana,' she said.

'It's lovely to meet you, Diana.'

She went even pinker. 'I loved you in *A Forever Kind of Love*.'

'Thank you,' he said. 'That's really kind of you.'

'Could, um, my friend be in the photo, too, please?' she asked.

He looked at Jess, who nodded and smiled. 'If you can show me how your camera works, I'll take the picture for you.'

When she'd taken the photo and Luke had signed autographs for both women and chatted to them for a little longer, he kissed Diana and her friend on the cheek. 'I think the dog's getting fidgety, if you'll excuse us,' he said with a smile. 'Enjoy the sunshine,' he said, and took Baloo's lead back from Jess.

'Does that happen a lot?' she asked, when the women were out of earshot. 'People coming up and asking for autographs and photos?'

'A bit. But it's fine.' Luke smiled. 'Without people going to see my films, I wouldn't have a job. The least I can do is spend a bit of time with them in return.'

Jess liked the fact that he was modest and appreciated the support of his fans. 'What about the paparazzi?'

'Most of the time, no. Only if there's some kind of story about me. They tend to follow the people in the news. And I'm very, very boring.'

Jess laughed. 'Is that my cue to tell you that you're terribly interesting and I'm dying to hear more about the history of London?'

He lifted his dark glasses for a second and gave her a speaking look. 'I'm wounded. *Wounded*, I tell you,' he said, clutching one hand theatrically to his chest.

She smiled, knowing that he was teasing. 'Actually, it *is* interesting, walking round with someone who can tell you what you're looking at.'

'Seriously, Jess, if I'm being boring, tell me to shut up. My ego can stand it.'

'I will. For now, you may go back to playing tour guide, Mr McKenzie,' she said with a smile.

'Just remember that you asked for that,' he said, laughing. 'OK. This is the Angel pub—there's been a pub on that spot for more than five hundred years. It's said that the captain of the *Mayflower* hired his crew there, and

Captain Cook planned his voyage to Australia there.'

A few minutes later, they came to the Mayflower pub. 'It's named after the ship, I imagine?' she asked.

'Yes. The pilgrims boarded it from the steps nearby—and it's the only place in England that's licensed to sell American postage stamps.'

'Seriously?'

He spread his hands. 'Seriously.'

'How do you know all this stuff?' she asked

He wrinkled his nose. 'Do you want the truth?'

She nodded.

'I've been on a few guided walks over the years. I've got quite a retentive memory, so I've mentally filed away all those little facts.'

'Of course—you're used to remembering things from learning lines.'

'I guess it's the same sort of thing. Learning a spiel, whether it's fact or fiction.'

Jess enjoyed strolling along the river as Luke pointed out various locations to her and told her the stories behind the sculptures.

'Joking apart, if you ever get bored with acting,' she said, 'I think you'd make quite a good tour guide. You really know your stuff.'

'Thank you.' He smiled. 'I'll bear that in mind.'

As they walked, her hand brushed against his a couple of times. It was totally accidental, but Jess felt as if little flames were licking underneath her skin every time they touched.

And then he twined his fingers through hers. For the life of her, she couldn't pull away.

Neither of them said a word, but Jess was intensely aware that she was strolling along the southern bank of the Thames in the brilliant sunshine, holding hands with someone who'd been voted the most beautiful man in the world. It just didn't seem possible; yet, at the same time, it felt incredibly real.

Luke only dropped her hand when they stopped at a park to give Baloo a drink. She took the opportunity to buy them both an ice cream, and they sat on the grass in the sunshine.

'It doesn't get any better than this. Early summer in England, with flowers out everywhere and bees buzzing lazily,' he said.

Was that a quote? Jess wondered. Not wanting to seem gauche, she didn't ask.

When they'd finished their ice cream, Luke stretched. 'Time to go back, I think.'

This time, when he held her hand, it was very deliberate.

Oh, help.

This felt a lot like old-fashioned courting.

How on earth was she going to explain it to her sister and her best friend—that she was sort of courting the actor they'd both had a huge crush on for years? How, for that matter, was she going to explain it to herself?

This couldn't have a future. Their lives were too different.

But maybe, she thought, maybe this was right for *just now*. No expectations, no promises—just enjoying the kind of closeness that both of them had missed.

They strolled back to his flat and sat on the balcony with a cold drink, enjoying the sunshine.

'I really enjoyed that walk,' she said. 'Thank you.'

'My pleasure.' His smile made her toes curl. He really was one of the most beautiful men she'd ever met; and yet he didn't behave as if he knew it. He was genuinely nice.

Why on earth had Fleur dumped him for someone else?

Not that she was going to ask. It wouldn't be tactful and she didn't want to hurt him by dragging up bad memories.

Eventually, she said, 'I guess I really ought to finish preparing dinner.'

There was a soft woof of agreement from beside them.

Jess laughed, and made a fuss of the Labrador. 'Sorry, curry isn't for dogs—but I did bring you something nice.' She fished in her pocket for a dog biscuit.

Luke smiled. 'I guess you have the tools of your trade on you all the time.'

She shrugged. 'Mine just happen to be visible. I bet you have large tracts of Shakespeare in your head.'

He spread his hands. 'I've spent half my life acting so, yes, I probably do.'

'What's your favourite Shakespeare?' she asked.

'Obviously I've got a soft spot for *Much Ado*, because it got me my big break. But my absolute favourite is probably *Macbeth*. I loved playing Macbeth. The "tomorrow and tomorrow and tomorrow" speech—it's so desolate. It squeezes my heart every time. How much he lost.' He smiled at her. 'What about you? What's your favourite?'

'I like *Much Ado*,' she said. 'Though I think probably everyone does because it's got a happy ending. My sister's an English teacher—she always makes me go to see *Twelfth Night* with her if it's on around Christmas. I always think the other characters are a bit too mean to Malvolio.' She flapped a dismissive hand. 'But I love the start of the play. "If music be the food of love…"'

'"Play on,"' Luke continued. '"Give me excess of it, that surfeiting, The appetite may sicken and so die. That strain again, it had a dying fall; O it came o'er my ear like the sweet sound That breathes upon a bank of violets, Stealing and giving odour. Enough; no more."'

Jess had closed her eyes so she could concentrate on the speech, enjoying the way he quoted. When he stopped, she opened her eyes again and looked at him. 'That was beautiful. Your voice is amazing.'

'Thank you.'

'Did you ever play Orsino?'

'Once. Though—' He wrinkled his nose. 'Well, it's the way he's in love with being in love. I don't have a lot of patience for him. I would much rather have played Feste, the jester. He's the most interesting clown in Shakespeare.'

There was something surreal about this conversation, Jess thought. 'I can't believe I'm talking Shakespeare with a world-famous actor,' she said. 'Especially as I don't really know what I'm talking about, and you do.'

'Actually, your views are just as valid as mine. Shakespeare wrote for his audience,' Luke said.

'But you've studied the plays. The characters. You know what they're all about.' And she'd bet her sister would love discussing Shakespeare with Luke. He'd probably enjoy talking about Shakespeare with Carly, too. They could argue about characters.

'It's my job,' he said. 'I wouldn't have a clue where to start with yours. I wouldn't even have been able to get Baloo to sit still, let alone dance.'

'You danced with her the other night,' she reminded him. 'Anyway. Dinner?'

'Let's go and sort it out. I'll be your sous chef.'

Again, Jess thought how surreal this was. How down-to-earth Luke was. He'd won several Oscars over the years and been nominated for still more—and yet here he was, offering to help her finish making the curry she'd cooked earlier.

He chopped the coriander and the cashews for her while she started preparing the rice and the broccoli. It was strange to work with someone in a kitchen again. It made her think of Matt, and all the times they'd cooked dinner together.

Luke said softly, 'Is this bringing back memories for you?'

'Yes,' she admitted. 'I'd forgotten how much I liked cooking with someone else.' She paused. 'And you?'

He shook his head. 'Fleur wasn't one for the kitchen. She'd rather eat out or get me to cook for us.' He smiled at her. 'And I can cook more than just stir fries. *Really* I can.'

'Yeah, yeah,' she teased back, glad that he'd lightened the atmosphere.

Once she'd finished serving up, he poured them both a glass of wine and ushered her up to the balcony.

'So what's in this?' he asked.

'You're a foodie, right?' she asked. At his nod, she said, 'You tell me.'

He tasted it. 'OK. Obviously coconut milk, green chillies, garlic, lime leaves, lime juice and coriander.' He thought about it a bit more. 'Fish sauce.'

'And?'

He shook his head. 'No. You've beaten me.'

'Lemongrass and galangal.'

He raised his eyebrows. 'This is where you tell me that you cheated and you used a paste from a jar.'

She laughed. 'No. I like cooking from scratch. I like the scent of fresh herbs and spices.'

'I should've taken you the other way on the river path, where all the spice warehouses were,' he said. 'They've all been made into luxury flats and swish eateries now, but the buildings still have the lovely old brickwork and the signs saying what each block was used for. So the story goes, when the buildings were first turned into flats, the first residents could still smell the spices that had been stored there over the past century.'

'That's a nice story, though I guess you'd have to like the scent of the particular spice from your building,' she said with a smile.

When they'd finished the meal and she'd oohed and aahed over the fabulous pavlova Luke had bought, Luke allowed her to help him take the crockery and cutlery downstairs, but flatly refused to let her wash up.

He made them both a mug of strong Italian roast coffee, and they drank it on the balcony, watching the boats go past on the river and seeing the lights go on in the buildings. At one point she stood up to lean on the balcony and get a better view of Tower Bridge; he joined her, his hand resting lightly on her shoulder. She wasn't sure which of them moved first, but then he was kissing her again, just as he'd kissed her last night.

This was when she should be sensible and stop this, she knew. When she should tell him they needed to go back to being just friends and colleagues. But the way he made her feel…

She'd forgotten just how much she liked kissing. Those little tiny nibbling kisses that sent flickers of desire up her spine. Teasing, promising, enticing. How could she resist?

She opened her mouth and let him deepen the kiss, and the flickers turned into flames.

When he broke the kiss, his pupils were huge, his mouth was slightly swollen and reddened, and there was a slash of colour across his cheekbones. She'd guess she was in the same state.

'Well,' he said softly. 'That wasn't supposed to happen.'

'We should be sensible,' she said.

He cupped her cheek, his fingers warm and gentle against her skin. 'Something about you makes me forget to be sensible, Jess.'

'Me, too,' she whispered, and leaned forward to kiss him.

This time, when she broke the kiss, he asked softly, 'Stay with me tonight?'

Stay with him.

She knew what he meant.

Spend the night with him. Make love. Share a part of herself that had been closed off for so long.

It was tempting. So very tempting.

But this was all happening so fast. They barely knew each other. They came from different worlds. He wasn't just a normal person she'd met at work—he was a film star. Talented, gorgeous, and seriously famous.

'I…'

He brushed his mouth against hers in the sweetest, gentlest kiss. 'I know. Too fast, too soon. And anyway…' His voice tailed off.

'What?' She hadn't seen him look nervous before.

He bit his lip. 'Jess, I like you, and I think you like me.'

She nodded, not quite trusting herself to speak. The 'but' was coming, she was sure of it.

'We haven't known each other that long.'

True.

'And it's way too early for us to have this conversation.'

'What conversation?' she asked carefully.

He sighed. 'It wouldn't be fair of me to let this thing between us carry on without you knowing all the facts. You need to go into this with your eyes wide open.' He paused. 'Set rules?' His expression was intense.

'Set rules,' she confirmed.

Saying it out loud felt like stepping off a ledge and not knowing how far he was going to fall. But Luke knew he owed it to Jess to be honest about this. 'I don't even know where to start,' he said. 'Whether to ask you or to tell you.'

She looked puzzled. 'Ask me or tell me what?'

'It's not tactful.' Especially after what she'd told him yesterday. 'But I owe you the truth.'

She reached over and took his hand. 'Telling someone something you've kept inside for a long time—it's hard. Like me telling you about…' Her voice wobbled slightly. 'About the baby. But, like you said to me, it's better out than in.'

He wasn't so sure. This could blow everything apart.

She said nothing more, just squeezed his hand and waited.

He dragged in a breath. 'I'm going to tell you something now that nobody else knows, not even Monica. Well, one other person knows, but…' Fleur didn't count, not any more. 'I can't have children.'

'And?'

He couldn't tell a thing from her expression. Whether it was a deal-breaker or not. But he'd started so he might as well finish. 'That's why Fleur and I broke up. I had mumps when I was a kid. It affected my fertility. So I couldn't give her a baby—at least, not without dragging her through IVF, and she was the one who'd have the burden of it, the one who'd have all the invasive medical stuff and have to take the drugs and what have you. And there are no guarantees it would work.' He swallowed hard. 'She wanted a baby, and that's why she went elsewhere. She had an affair with someone who could give her a child. She got pregnant, and that's when I found out about the affair, because the baby obviously wasn't mine. I could've forgiven her, raised the child as mine—but then she told me that she'd only been with me in the first place because she thought it would further her career. She'd never really loved me.'

Jess moved closer. Giving him strength, the way he'd done for her. 'I don't know your ex,' she said, 'but I can't believe anyone could be so selfish and cruel. What she did was—well, words fail me. That's so horrible.' She looked angry, Luke thought—just like she had when she'd taken him to task over the dog, the day he'd first met her. 'Right now I want to shake the woman until her teeth rattle. It's not your fault that you had mumps as a child. How could she hurt you like that?'

'She wanted a baby. Desperately,' he said. 'And I couldn't do that for her.'

'IVF isn't the only way to have a child. There's adoption, fostering. She didn't give you a chance, Luke. And to have an affair, to cheat on you and only think about what she wanted...' She shook her head. 'I don't get it. If you love someone, you make the effort and you talk to each other and you work out a compromise.'

That was what he'd thought, too. 'It's not tactful of me to ask this. Not when yesterday...' He bit his lip. 'Jess, I'd like to get to know you better. A lot better. But I know you were planning to have children. You need to know that I can't do that for you, if we're going to be together. It was a deal-breaker for Fleur.'

'I'm not Fleur,' she pointed out.

He didn't quite dare hope. Because there was another barrier, too. 'And I'm not sure I can live up to Matt. He sounds like an incredible guy.'

'He was, but that isn't quite the way things work,' Jess said. 'You're different people. You have different qualities. It's not fair to compare you and I'm not going to do that.'

'So where,' Luke asked, 'does this leave us?'

'I don't know. I'm just an ordinary woman,' she said.

There was nothing ordinary about Jess Greenacre, Luke thought.

'And you're a film star. People come up to you in the street and ask you for autographs.'

'Is that a problem?'

'Of course not.' She shook her head. 'It's part of your job—part of who you are. But I'm not Hollywood material. I'm not sure I'd fit in to that world.'

'Everyone likes you on set, so that's a pretty good indicator,' he pointed out.

'Mimi doesn't like me.'

He smiled, then. 'That's because you're female. Don't take it personally. She's definitely not the litmus test.' He took her hand. 'I like you. I think you like me. I'd like to see where this goes. So if you can handle the fact that my life can be a bit chaotic, the press can be intrusive, and I can't give you a child—well, not without a lot of medical intervention, and there aren't any guarantees it would happen for us anyway—then maybe we can make this work.'

'There are no guarantees about anything,' Jess said. 'I've learned that over the last year or so.' She took a deep breath. 'So. Me, you and Baloo.'

The dog wagged her tail hopefully.

'Me, you—and Baloo,' Luke echoed. 'Don't decide now. Think about it. I'll take you home, and we'll talk about it again tomorrow.'

'OK. We'll talk tomorrow,' Jess said.

Luke drove her home and was utterly restrained, merely kissing her goodbye on the cheek and waiting in the car until she was safely indoors. She needed to make this decision with a clear head, not when he'd swept her off her feet. He wanted her to make the right choice for *her*.

He just hoped she'd make the same decision he wanted, too.

CHAPTER TEN

JESS THOUGHT ABOUT it. And thought about it some more.

Luke had been honest with her. Totally open.

If she chose to see where this took them, her whole life would change. She'd be dating someone in the public eye. Everything they did would be reported. Sometimes it would be twisted, simply to sell a news story, totally disregarding their feelings. Luke had admitted that sometimes he just had to suck it up and ignore it.

Having a child together could involve yet more intrusiveness, either through medical procedures or through being vetted by an adoption agency: things that would put a strain on any relationship.

And Jess had to be honest: she did want a family, at some point in the future.

But then there was Luke himself. Luke,

who'd made her smile again. Luke, who'd given her strength. Luke, who'd listened and who was taking her feelings into account, not expecting her just to drop everything to suit him. Luke, who made her heart beat faster every time she saw him, and not just because he was a handsome movie star with the charm and charisma that went with the job description. It was the man, not the image, that drew her.

Should she say yes? Take the risk?

Or should she play it super-safe and say no?

In the end, she slept on it.

And she woke smiling, thinking of Luke.

That decided her. She grabbed her mobile phone and texted him. *Made my decision.*

Five minutes later, her phone rang.

'Hi,' Luke said. 'I got your text. How did you sleep?'

'Surprisingly well,' she said. 'You?'

'Not answering that one,' he said. 'So you've thought about it?'

'Yes.'

'And?'

'Are you still sure you want to do this?' She needed to know it was still the same for him.

'I'm sure. And you?'

'There are no guarantees. But I do know that I don't want to be sitting here in thirty years' time, wondering what might have been if I'd been brave enough to say yes.'

'Is that an incredibly roundabout way of saying yes, Ms Greenacre?' Luke asked.

'Let me see. That would be…' She paused just long enough to hear him groan. 'Yes.'

'Can Baloo and I come and see you?'

'Yes.'

'Good. Get ready. We'll go out somewhere for lunch.'

On a proper date.

Their first real date as a couple.

'See you soon,' she said.

Showering and washing her hair didn't take long. Deciding what to wear took a lot longer. And then she shook herself. Luke wasn't dating her because of her dress sense. He could've dated a dozen A-list actresses with much better wardrobes than hers. He was dating her because he liked her for herself.

She opted for smart trousers and a pretty summery top. And she was just about ready when the doorbell rang.

Luke stood on her doorstep with an armful of flowers—beautiful summer flowers, bright pink germini, violet-coloured agapanthus, white roses and tiny chrysanthemums.

She looked at them and smiled. 'They're beautiful. Thank you. I'll put them in water.'

He smiled back. 'I thought the chrysanthemums might be appropriate from me. They're called charms.'

'Charming flowers from a charming man.' She liked the wordplay. 'That's great. Can I get you some coffee?'

'No. I thought we could go out for a walk. It's your turn to play tour guide.'

'Bad luck. I don't know this part of London that well,' she said.

He took his phone out of his pocket. 'All righty. We do it the cheat's way. Internet.'

'You really do have an answer for everything, don't you?' she asked.

He spread his hands. 'I try.'

Thanks to the Internet, they found directions to a nearby park, and Jess thoroughly enjoyed sitting in the sun, making a fuss of Baloo. And they managed to find a pub with a dog-friendly garden, so they could eat lunch with the dog sitting patiently under the table.

But when they returned to her flat, Jess hadn't even opened the door when someone walked up the path behind them and coughed. 'Mrs Greenacre. May I remind you that your lease doesn't allow for dogs?'

Oh, no. So her neighbour had talked to their landlord. 'I'm sorry, Mr Bright,' she said.

'Actually, it's my fault,' Luke said. 'I'm

looking after Baloo and I can't leave her on her own. I do hope it's not a problem that she's here temporarily.'

Jess's landlord frowned. 'Don't I know you from somewhere?'

'Luke, this is Mr Bright, my landlord. Mr Bright, this is my friend Luke McKenzie,' Jess introduced them dutifully.

'I *knew* I knew you from somewhere! You're my wife's favourite actor. She loves your films. Could I have your autograph for her?'

'With pleasure,' Luke said. 'I can send a signed photo via Jess tomorrow, if you like.'

'That'd really make her day.'

The landlord had moved from slightly aggressive to cheerfully pally, Jess thought with relief. Being a movie star definitely had its plus points.

'What's her name?' Luke asked.

'Mary.'

'Spelled the usual way?' Luke checked. At the landlord's nod, he smiled and made a note in his phone. 'I'll send the photo through Jess.'

'Thank you. Mrs Greenacre, if you could kindly remember the rule, no permanent dogs. But I suppose this one can visit, as long as it's only for a little while,' Mr Bright said. 'No chewing or messing, mind you.'

'I guarantee it,' Luke said.

'That's all right, then. Good day to you.'

Inside Jess's flat, they looked at each other and then burst out laughing.

'I'm sorry,' she said. 'That has to be…'

He flapped a dismissive hand. 'It's fine. I'm the one breaching the rules of your lease.'

'Ah, but we have a temporary permit for Baloo.' Jess made a fuss of the dog. 'So we're fine. Let's get you a drink, girl, and I'll put the kettle on. Go and make yourself at home, Luke.'

He noticed that she'd put the photograph frames up on the mantelpiece. So she'd listened to what he'd said. And when she came in bearing two mugs of coffee, the dog trotting at her heels, he didn't say a word. He just hugged her. Just because.

Over the next week, Jess's world got better and better. She enjoyed her job, even though she was rushed off her feet; she loved having the dog with her all day; and she spent most of her evenings with Luke. Apart from Thursday, when Luke's aunt was finally due home from America and he wanted to meet her from the airport, so Jess arranged to meet her best friend for a drink after work.

Shannon walked into the bar where they'd agreed to meet, did a double take and then said, 'You're glowing. Have you met someone?'

Hmm. How could she tell her best friend that she was seeing Luke McKenzie? 'Sort of.'

'Good.' Shannon smiled. 'It'll do you good, and I knew Matt well so I can say with perfect honesty that he wouldn't have wanted you to shut yourself up in a mausoleum after he died. He would've wanted you to find someone who loves you as much as he did and really live your life to the full.'

'Uh-huh.'

'What's his name? Where did you meet him? When do I get to meet him?'

'That's a lot of questions,' Jess said.

'Which you're obviously not going to answer.' Shannon rolled her eyes. 'I should've trained as a dentist instead of becoming a teacher.'

'Why?'

'Because getting information out of you is like pulling teeth.'

Jess laughed. 'It's not that bad. Look, Shan,

it's early days. I don't want to jinx things or rush things.'

'OK. I won't push you any more. But, just so you know, everyone will be pleased for you and nobody's going to say it's too soon or anything stupid like that.' Shannon hugged her. 'We all worry about you being alone.'

Jess raised an eyebrow. 'There's nothing wrong with being single.'

'I know that, honey. That's not what I meant—I don't think you have to be part of a couple to be a valid person. I just worry that you've shut yourself off from life since Matt and Comet were killed. It's good that you've met someone who makes you smile again.'

'Yes, he does.'

'So when do we get to meet him?'

Oh, boy. That would be a meeting and a half. 'Soon,' Jess prevaricated. 'As I said, it's very early days.'

'OK. I won't nag. Even though I'm completely eaten up with curiosity and I have a million and one questions I'm dying to ask. You look happy, and that's enough for me.'

Jess just hugged her. 'Thank you.'

On Friday morning, Luke said, 'So how was last night?'

'Good,' she said. 'How was your aunt?'

'Settling in again.' He smiled. 'Have dinner with me tonight?'

She nodded. 'Thanks. I'd like that.'

'Except,' he said, 'it's a takeaway, and it's not at mine—it's at Monica's.'

He was taking her to meet his aunt? The one he was close to—the one who'd rescued Baloo. Panic flooded through her. OK, so they were officially an item now; but they were keeping it low-profile and they were careful to be professional whenever they met on set.

Meeting the family was tantamount to a declaration of intent.

As if Luke guessed the direction of her thoughts, he said, 'Relax. She just wants to meet you because you've been looking after Baloo. She wants to say thank you herself. It isn't a big deal.'

Jess wasn't so sure. She bought a bouquet of cheerful sunflowers, then had second thoughts when Luke came into the production office at the end of filming. 'Luke, is it OK to take flowers to your aunt?'

'Yes.' He looked at them and smiled. 'She'll love them.'

This time, rather than driving them towards the Thames, he drove them to Notting Hill. Another wealthy part of London,

Jess thought. Again she was aware that Luke wasn't just wealthy in his own right, he came from quite a privileged background—one so different from her own, vastly normal background.

The first thing that struck Jess when Luke let them into the house and introduced her to Monica was how like Luke she looked. 'I, um—it's very nice to meet you,' she said, feeling ridiculously shy, and cross with herself for feeling that way.

'And you. Thank you for the flowers. They're beautiful. Luke, can you put them in water for me?' Monica asked.

'And arrange the takeaway. Sure. Chinese OK with you, Jess?' he asked.

'It'll be lovely, thanks.'

She made polite small talk with Monica while Luke was in the kitchen. When he came back, he said, 'Jess, are you going to show Mon what you've taught Baloo?'

'I—well, if you think I should.'

'Definitely.'

Feeling even more nervous, Jess switched on the music and took Baloo through their routine.

'That's incredible,' Monica said, making a fuss of the dog. 'So clever.'

'I can't take all the credit,' Jess said. 'It was

a little girl in the park who gave me the idea. I was giving Baloo some basic training, and the little girl said she'd seen a dancing dog on the television and asked me if I was going to teach Baloo to dance. I gave it a go and it turns out she's a natural.'

'She's a very clever girl indeed.' Monica gave Luke a speaking look. 'She'd fit well into a showbiz life.'

'We've had this conversation,' Luke reminded her. 'And don't you gang up with her, Jess.'

'As if I would,' Jess said, and gave him a wicked grin.

The ice was thoroughly broken, and Jess told Monica about some of the training work and exhibitions she'd done.

'I wanted to say thank you,' Monica said, when Luke took Baloo out into the garden. 'For making Luke smile again.'

'Me? I haven't done anything,' Jess said.

'Hmm.' Monica looked unconvinced. 'OK, so you're keeping it between yourselves for now. Fair enough.'

Jess felt the colour flood into her face. Oh, help.

Monica patted her hand. 'I won't tell him I know. Even though he must know I would've guessed.'

'I know you're close to him,' Jess said. 'He talks about you a lot.' And he said hardly anything about his parents.

'He's the best nephew I could've had,' Monica said.

'The only nephew, according to him.'

'He's the nearest I have to a child of my own, and I love him dearly.' Monica sighed. 'Much as I love my sister Erica, she wouldn't win any prizes for maternal feeling.'

Jess, knowing that this was immensely private, said softly, 'Set rules.'

'Set rules? Oh—what you hear and what you see stays with you.' Monica nodded. 'Thank you. Let's just say that Luke grew up in a house with white carpets.'

'High maintenance,' Jess said, wondering how his mother would have reacted to the inevitable spills.

'You can say that again. He grew up disappointing her. And his father.' Monica rolled her eyes. 'Even now they'd like him to give up his acting and go back to being a lawyer, so he'd fit in to their expectations of him.'

'He would've made a good barrister. He's meticulous and he's got stage presence,' Jess pointed out.

'True,' Monica said.

'But you're right—it wouldn't have made

him happy.' Jess sighed. 'I come from a materially much poorer background, but I think I was the lucky one. My parents said that as long as my sister and I were happy in what we did, then they were happy—that was all they wanted.'

'Very sensible,' Monica said. 'I agree with them.' She grimaced. 'I wasn't able to have children myself, so I was always happy to borrow Luke and do messy stuff with him at my place—painting, glitter and glue, play dough and making cupcakes with icing and sprinkles.'

'And I bet you supported him when he said he wanted to act,' Jess said.

'It was the first time I'd seen him really come alive,' Monica said. 'Of course I was going to support him. He'd found the thing of his heart. So I ran interference with his parents as much as I could.' She smiled. 'I still do. His mother's always giving dinner parties where he can meet someone suitable.'

Luke's parents are definitely *not* going to approve of me, Jess thought.

Either she'd said it aloud or Luke's aunt was immensely perceptive, because Monica said softly, 'It doesn't matter what they think about you, it matters what Luke thinks about you—and right now he's happier than I've seen him in a very, very long time.'

It was the same for Jess. But right now she didn't want to talk about that. 'I was going to ask you about Baloo. Were all the kennels really full?'

'No,' Monica admitted, 'and I was taking a huge risk.'

'Giving a rescue dog with special needs to a total novice—that could really have blown up in your face, Monica. Big time.'

Monica laughed. 'I like you, Jess. You tell it like it is and yes, you're right. It could have blown up in my face. Especially as I wasn't here to rescue them if it went wrong.' She glanced ruefully at her cast. 'And especially as this happened. I hate being stuck in a cast and having to rely on other people to do even basic stuff for me.'

'That's what Luke said—he'd give you a day of being in hospital before you were climbing the walls.'

'He got that right,' Monica said wryly.

'Got what right?' Luke asked, coming in to hear the tail end of the conversation.

'Being stuck in hospital drove me crazy. At least I can do things, now I'm home.'

'Just promise me you'll be sensible and ask

me for help when you need it,' Luke said. 'And I mean that, Mon.'

She rolled her eyes. 'Don't fuss. I'm fine.'

'I mean it,' Luke said. 'Otherwise I'll let my dog loose on your shoe cupboard.'

Monica exchanged a glance with Jess and smiled. And Jess knew exactly why the older woman was smiling: Luke was definitely near to accepting Baloo as his permanent dog.

Jess felt as if their relationship had turned a corner; over the next week, she and Luke grew closer, and she was really starting to think that, despite the huge differences between their lives, this might just work for both of them.

On Saturday night, she was sitting on the balcony with him, wrapped in his arms, when he nuzzled her ear. 'Stay with me tonight, Jess.'

Stay with him.

Her pulse skipped a beat, and then another.

Stay with him. Fall asleep in his arms, and wake up with him.

Part of her wanted to. Yet part of her was scared. It had been a long time. Supposing she disappointed him? 'I—I don't have anything with me,' she prevaricated.

He shrugged. 'Well, I have a spare toothbrush and a washing machine. And, although I probably can't produce anything like moisturiser, you're very welcome to use whatever you need in the bathroom.'

'You make it sound so easy,' she whispered.

'It *is* easy.' He kissed her. 'Stay, Jess. No pressure. We don't have to do anything you don't want to do. You can use the spare room if you'd rather.'

Time to meet him halfway, Jess thought. 'I want to stay.'

'But?'

'It's been a while,' she said. 'What if I disappoint you?'

'You won't disappoint me. Ever,' he said.

And it really was that easy.

Baloo, for once, stayed on her own bed when she was told, and didn't do her usual trick of opening the door and escaping upstairs.

And Jess discovered that Luke's bedroom had the best view in the house. When she told him, he laughed and pulled the blind. 'I have a better one right now.'

He undressed her slowly, gently, stroking every inch of skin as he uncovered it. Jess in turn enjoyed taking his clothes off, discovering how soft his skin was, finding out where he liked being touched and how she could make him gasp with pleasure.

'Just so you know, I wasn't taking this for granted,' Luke said as he removed a condom from his wallet. 'And the Press seriously over-report how many women I sleep with.'

She liked the fact that he'd guessed at some of her reservations—and he'd guessed correctly. But she also wanted to keep this light. So neither of them would feel pressured. 'Are you trying to tell me you have a stunt double for Most Beautiful Man in the World, Mr McKenzie?' she teased.

He groaned. 'That accolade's very flattering, but I'm not sure I live up to their expectations. They haven't seen me first thing in the morning, with bed hair and stubble and being grumpy before my first cup of coffee.' He stole a kiss. 'You've been warned, by the way.'

'Noted,' she said, and let him carry her to his bed.

The next morning, Jess woke feeling sated and happier than she'd felt in a long, long time.

'Morning.' Luke drew her closer and kissed her. 'OK?'

'Very OK.' She snuggled against him. 'I

thought you said you looked a mess and were grumpy, first thing?'

'Bed hair, stubble, shadows under my eyes because I didn't get a lot of sleep last night...'

She laughed. 'You know, if the award-givers could see you right now...' She stole a kiss. 'They'd cancel all future awards on the grounds that nobody could look as good as this ever again.'

'I wasn't fishing.'

'And I wasn't flattering,' she said softly. 'You're beautiful, Luke.'

'And so,' he said, 'are you.'

She scoffed. 'Come off it. I'm ordinary. You work with some of the most gorgeous women in the world.'

'Most of which is achieved with make-up and good lighting. It isn't real. You are. And it's not just about looks. It's about how you make me feel.' He kissed her. 'Waking up with you, I don't feel grumpy and in need of coffee. I'm with you, so I know it's going to be a glorious day.'

It was one of the nicest compliments Jess had ever been paid, and she felt her face go pink with pleasure. 'Thank you.' And it was the same for her. Being with him had taught her how to be happy again.

He kissed her again. 'Much as I want to do

all sorts of wicked things with you right now, I have a dog who needs to go out and who's probably trashed my kitchen cupboards because I turned the door handle upside down so she had to stay put last night.' He rolled his eyes. 'Stay there. I'll make us a coffee while I clear up.'

'Are you sure you don't want a hand?'

'I'm sure.'

Jess lay back against the deep pillows and drowned until Luke appeared in the doorway with two mugs of coffee. A second later there was a flying leap and a thud as Baloo landed on the bed.

'So how was your kitchen?' she asked Luke as she made a fuss of the dog.

'Perfect,' he said. 'I was expecting rice and pasta everywhere. She hadn't opened a single door or chewed a single packet.'

Because, Jess thought, the dog was finally feeling secure. She knew she was *home*.

'Good girl,' Jess said, and made a fuss of the dog.

'You don't mind?' Luke asked, gesturing to Baloo.

She smiled. 'This was how Sunday mornings were at home if we weren't on duty. Coffee, the papers, and lazing the morning away in bed with Comet snoring his head off at the bottom of the bed.'

His eyes widened for a moment. 'I didn't think. Sorry. I'll—'

'No, it's fine,' Jess said. 'They're happy memories. Like you said, it's part of who I am.' She kissed him lightly. 'And, like you said, it's going to be a glorious day.'

Over the next couple of weeks, Jess ended up staying most of the time at Luke's house, only dropping back to hers occasionally to pick up fresh clothes. The one day she did stay at home was when she'd been in court to testify at the hearing of the man who'd mugged her, and Luke had planned to pick up Baloo from Monica before meeting Jess at her flat.

When the doorbell went, Jess rushed to answer it—and was surprised to see her sister standing there. 'Oh—Carly!'

'Is now not a good time?' Carly asked.

'No, it's fine. I just wasn't expecting you, that's all.'

Carly raised her eyebrows. 'Well, you've been so unavailable lately, I just wanted to call round and check you were actually OK.'

'I'm fine.' Jess hugged her sister. 'Come in. I'll put the kettle on.'

Hopefully Luke would end up chatting to

Monica and running late, and Carly would
be gone by the time he arrived. Much as
Jess loved her sister, she wasn't quite ready
to admit that she was seeing Luke. This was
all still too new.

But Carly was in the mood to talk, and
when the doorbell went again Jess knew that
it was Luke.

'It's probably a neighbour with a parcel delivery or something,' she fibbed, and went to
answer the door.

'My sister's here,' she told Luke.

He raised an eyebrow. 'Is that a problem?
Will she think it's too soon for you to be seeing someone?'

'I—um…'

'Jessie, is everything all right?' Carly came
out into the hallway and gasped as she saw
who was standing at the front door. 'Oh, my
God! Luke McKenzie.'

'You must be Carly. Lovely to meet you.'
He held out his hand to shake hers.

'I—you—oh, my God,' Carly said again.

'I should be recording this,' Jess said.
'The first time our Carly's ever been lost for
words.'

Carly cuffed her. 'Luke McKenzie,' she
said again.

'And Baloo.' He introduced the dog to her.

'Though I imagine you know all about her, as Jess has been looking after her for me.'

'She has?' Carly stared at the dog and then at Jess, who was making a fuss of the dog. 'You said you were working on a film set.'

'I am. I'm in the production team,' Jess said. 'One of my duties is looking after the leading actor's dog and stopping her munching on expensive designer shoes. Luke, come in. I'll get you a coffee.'

'Thank you,' He kissed her lingeringly.

Jess felt her face flame. If Carly had been under any illusions that her relationship with Luke was strictly professional, they were well and truly blown, now. Because that most definitely hadn't been a business kiss or an actor's air kiss.

Carly appeared to have recovered herself. 'Come and sit down, Luke. As Jess said, she'll make coffee.'

'Carly,' Jess began, but her sister shooed her away, clearly in bossy teacher mode.

'Sorry,' she mouthed at Luke, and went to make coffee at double speed.

'So you're seeing my little sister,' Carly said.

'Yes. Is that a problem?' Luke asked.

'I hope not.' Carly folded her arms. 'I don't

mean to be rude, but I'm her big sister and it's my job to look out for her.'

As an only child, Luke didn't have a clue about sibling relationships. But he liked the fact that Carly obviously loved her sister very much and worried about her.

'Has she told you about last year?' Carly asked.

Straight to the point. Luke liked that, too. 'About Matt and Comet?' He nodded. 'She trusted me with that much. And…' He gestured to the mantelpiece.

'She's finally put the photos back.' Carly's eyes filmed with tears. 'Was that anything to do with you?'

Jess clearly hadn't mentioned the mugging or the trial today, and it wasn't his place to tell Carly about it. 'A bit,' he said. 'And I want you to know that I have no intention of hurting your sister.'

'Good. Jess has been in a bad place and I don't want her going back there. Ever again.'

'She won't be there on my account,' he assured her.

'Thank you—and she seems to be bonding with your dog.'

'Temporary dog,' he corrected. 'Once my aunt's back on her feet, she's going to find Baloo a proper home.'

Carly looked at him. 'Hmm. I know a good home—and I also know that Jess's lease is up in a couple of months. There's no reason why she can't find another place that *will* allow her to have a dog.'

He smiled. 'She said you'd nagged her about her job.'

'She hated it, Luke—she was so miserable, and even now she refuses to go to our parents' house because she can't face seeing the dog. She makes them come here or sees them at mine. Maybe now that will change.' She bit her lip. 'I know Mum and Dad understand—we've all been worried about her. We all think this new job has been good for her, but she kept it quiet that she was looking after your dog.'

'Maybe she needs time to work things out for herself,' Luke suggested. 'And you do know she'd be cross with both of us for talking about her.'

'Yes, I am,' Jess said, walking into the room in time to overhear the last bit. 'Don't talk about me. I'm a grown-up and I can make my own decisions.'

Carly spread her hands, 'Jessie, I love you, and you know we've all worried ourselves sick about you since Matt died.'

'I'm fine,' Jess said. 'Really.'

'I think,' Carly said, 'I believe you. For the first time in months.'

'Good. Shut up and drink your coffee.' She scowled at Carly. 'You were supposed to be so dazzled at meeting your idol that you'd stay lost for words.'

Luke laughed. 'No way is your sister ever going to be lost for words, Jess.'

'Charming.' Carly rolled her eyes, but she was laughing. 'I still can't quite take in that my sister's dating a movie star—oh, and thank you for the signed photos, Luke. Shannon and I both appreciated it.'

'My pleasure.' He smiled at her. 'I know you're an English teacher. Jess tells me you take her to see *Twelfth Night* every year.'

Carly nodded. 'I can imagine you as Orsino.'

He smiled. 'Yes, I've done that. But I want to play Feste.'

'Can you sing?'

He launched into Feste's song from the end of the play.

'That,' Carly said when he'd finished, 'was lovely. Did you ever think about auditioning for *Les Mis*?'

'My singing voice isn't good enough, not for a full-blown musical,' Luke said. 'Though

I have to admit I'd love to do *The Sound of Music*.'

'Captain von Trapp.' Carly grinned. 'Yes. I can see that. You've got that lovely rich voice, like Christopher Plummer. You know, you might be the only person who could do a better Captain von Trapp than him.'

Jess groaned. 'Luke, just make her the head of your fan club now, will you?'

He laughed. 'I don't have a fan club. But thank you both for the compliment.'

The conversation turned to favourite films and plays. Carly and Luke were both animated, and Jess thought how well Luke fitted in to this side of her life. Maybe, just maybe, this was going to work out.

'I ought to go,' Carly said finally. 'Jessie, see me out?'

Jess knew what her sister meant. Time to be grilled.

She went to the front door with Carly.

'Shannon said you were seeing someone, but she didn't push you for details because she didn't want you to go back into your shell. I can't believe it's Luke McKenzie.' Carly smiled. 'You're right—he lives up to all my expectations and Shannon's. He's fabulous.'

'Are you going to tell her?'

'That's your place, love, not mine.'

Luke walked into the hallway and overheard the last bit. 'Let's make it easier. Why don't both of you come for dinner at my place on Saturday? Bring your husband—and Shannon can bring hers, too.'

'Oh, my God. Luke, I'm so sorry. I wasn't angling for an invite,' Carly said, looking aghast.

'I know, but Jess is close to you, and of course you want to know more about the person she's seeing.' Luke looked at her. 'Invite your parents, too, Jess. We'll eat in the garden if it's good weather.'

This was it: they'd be outing their relationship as a real one. It was a huge step. For both of them.

'Are you sure about this?' she asked.

'I'm sure.' He paused. 'Are you?'

She nodded. 'I think so.'

When Carly had gone, Jess said again, 'Are you really sure about this?'

'Yes.'

'You've invited my parents—what about yours?'

He shook his head. 'I'm not ready for you to meet them—and that's not because I'm ashamed of you or anything remotely like it, but because my parents are a bit difficult and I think we need some time to get used to this thing between us before you meet them.'

She thought about what Monica said about his mother always being disappointed in him and it didn't matter what his parents thought about her, it mattered what Luke thought. Not that she was going to tell him, because she didn't want him to feel she'd been gossiping about him. Even though he'd been gossiping about her with her sister.

'But I will invite Monica,' Luke said. 'The bathroom and garden are both on the ground floor, so she won't have to negotiate stairs.'

'What if it rains?' Jess asked.

He smiled. 'We'll all just have to pile into my office. Or I can really annoy Mon by playing the superhero and carrying her upstairs.'

Everyone was free on Saturday. And Luke made everyone feel totally at home rather than that they were trespassing in a movie star's pad.

He talked Jess into doing the performance she'd choreographed with Baloo, and everyone sang along with the song—and then made a huge fuss of the dog, who was in a state of utter bliss from all the attention.

Monica and Jess exchanged a glance. They both knew that Baloo had definitely found her permanent home. Luke just needed to realise that, too.

At the end of the evening, Jess's parents dropped her home. 'He's lovely,' Jess's mother said.

'And he's good for you, which is the most important thing for us. We like him,' Jess's father added.

'Yes. Luke's special,' Jess said, smiling.

They'd cleared the first hurdle with ease.

So maybe, just maybe, this was going to work out just fine.

'She's lovely,' Monica said to Luke when everyone had gone. 'And she's good for you. She loves dogs. She's perfect.'

He grimaced. 'Mon, it's still early days.'

'I know, love,' she reassured him. 'The fact you've introduced her to me, and you asked me here when you met her family and best friend, tells me a lot. I like her.' She gave him a hug. 'I think she makes you happy, and you make her happy. And that's all that matters.'

CHAPTER ELEVEN

THE DOORBELL RANG insistently.

Luke, presuming that it was a delivery of some sort, opened the front door. To his shock, flashlights started going off in his face and microphones were shoved at him. There were people six deep on the doorstep, all talking at once, and the noise was incredible.

'So is it true?' one of them called.

Uh-oh. If he was being papped, that could only mean one thing. Another story. A juicy one, this time. Had Fleur found out somehow that he was seeing someone, and implied to her tame journo that it was a relationship that predated the end of their marriage, to let her off the hook of her own perfidy? Oh, hell. If that was the case, he'd need to handle this quickly and carefully to make sure that Jess didn't get hurt.

'No comment,' he said, and closed the door. The doorbell rang again, but this time he ignored it. Instead, he grabbed his phone and flicked into the Internet to look at the news gossip pages and find out exactly what was going on before he called the publicity team at the film company and asked them to start damage limitation.

The headline leapt out at him: *Luke Mc-Manly?*

Oh, God, no.

The story wasn't about Jess, but that was small comfort. Because now the one thing Luke had spent the last year worrying about had actually happened.

Someone had broken the story about his infertility. And now the press was saying he was less of a man because he couldn't father a child.

He scrolled through the story, his temper simmering more and more as he read. He wasn't sure what made him angriest—the invasion of his privacy, or the way the gossip rag implied that the reason he'd not done as well in his last film was because he'd played a father and, not being able to become a father himself, hadn't been able to get into the role properly. His personal life had got in the way of his job.

What made it worse was his inner fear that there was some truth in it. That maybe he hadn't done as well in the role because he couldn't identify with what it was like to be a father. That he'd done his research and knew what it would be like intellectually, but he hadn't managed to transfer it emotionally. He hadn't been able to feel it—or make his audience feel it.

Life on set was going to be unbearable. People would be whispering in corners and then going silent as soon as they saw him. Pitying him. And they'd make the connection with Fleur and pity him even more.

Luke *hated* this.

And right now there was a pack of journalists and photographers waiting outside his front door. No doubt there would be a gaggle of them at the entrance to the set, too. This was a nightmare. Just like it had been when he'd split up with Fleur; he'd been shadowed every minute of the day and everyone had wanted to dig, dig, dig into his private life and his feelings.

As if Baloo could sense his mood, she whined and lay on her back at his feet.

'It's not you, girl,' he said.

He couldn't take the dog out through the back gate; it would mean having to take her on public transport during the rush hour. So they were going to have to drive out of the garage at the front of the house, as they normally did, and he'd have to hope that the paparazzi were sensible enough to get out of his way.

Thank God he always reversed into his garage rather than driving straight in.

He put the dog in her crate in the back of the car, put a pair of dark glasses on as he got behind the wheel of the car, then opened the garage door with the remote control.

The photographers crowded round him as the door opened, bulbs flashing everywhere. He opened his side window just enough to tell them to get out of his way or he'd call the police and have them removed from the street for causing a public obstruction.

One of them made a snippy comment and his temper snapped. 'Or maybe it'd be quicker to just drive over the lot of you,' he snarled.

By the time he got to the set the pictures were on the Internet from this morning—describing him as 'mean and moody'. And there was a headline to go with it: *Un-Daddy Un-Cool.*

The scumbags, he thought, gritting his teeth. They were so busy thinking of snarky words and poking fun at people, congratulating themselves on their cleverness, that they ignored the fact there was actually a person behind the story. Someone who could get hurt.

Sticks and stones may break my bones… The old rhyme ran through his head. And how wrong it was. Because names could hurt. Words could cut deeper than anything else, seeping into your head and freezing you.

This was a total nightmare. Luke was used to press conferences and interviews and photographs, but he hated this side of the business—the muck-raking and the way the press acted as if the public owned you and you had to live every last little detail of your life under the glare of a photographer's flashlight.

As he walked onto the set, Luke could tell that everyone had seen the article. The way they stopped talking as soon as they saw him, the pitying glances. He did his best to ignore it and walked into the production office—but even Jess was looking anxious when she saw him, treating him with kid gloves.

He couldn't handle this. Jess was the one person he'd told about this, the one person he'd expected to understand—and yet she was behaving like all the rest of them, pitying him.

'Are you OK?' she asked.

His temper finally snapped. 'Of course I'm not OK! My private life's being dragged through the gutter yet again. How the hell do you think I feel?'

Her face went white. And then she lifted her chin. 'Does it not occur to you that maybe I'm concerned about you?'

Luke knew that he was completely in the wrong, but he couldn't stop himself. His mouth was on a roll. All the pent-up anger and bitterness of the last year poured out of him. 'Maybe I don't need your concern. Maybe I don't *want* your concern.' And then the words he knew he shouldn't say came out anyway. 'Maybe I'm better off on my own. Without you.'

She flinched as if he'd struck her physically. 'If that's the way you feel,' she said quietly, 'then you probably are.' She looked over at Ayesha, the production manager. 'I'm sorry to let you down, but I'm afraid I can't work today.'

And then she simply picked up her things and walked out.

Baloo whined and tugged at her lead, desperate to be with Jess, but Luke didn't move a muscle to stop Jess leaving. Even though he knew he was in the wrong and should apologise, he was too angry to focus on anything else but how he felt right at that moment. He glared at the dog. 'You'll have to be on set with me today, and if you so much as look at a single shoe, let alone steal one and chew it, you're going back to the dogs' home as fast as I can drive you there.'

'Mr McKenzie,' Ayesha said, 'just leave the dog with me for now.'

The cool, clipped tone of her voice registered, and he looked at the production manager.

'Baloo's used to me,' Ayesha said. 'She'll be fine.'

Luke was about to thank her when she cut in. 'It's none of my business,' she said, 'but I think you've just made the biggest mistake of your life.'

'No, I don't think so,' he said coldly. Because maybe he *was* better off on his own. And, from this evening, his aunt would just have to pay someone to look after Baloo until she could find the dog a new home. He didn't need anything or anyone in his life. Not now, not ever.

Anger kept Jess going until she was inside her flat. Sure, she could understand that Luke was angry and hurt by the story—but that didn't give him the right to take it out on her. Would this be what their life would've been like had they stayed together, Luke going off at the deep end whenever something upset him in the press? She didn't want to have to spend the rest of her life treading on eggshells. She wanted an equal partnership, like the one she'd had with Matt. Of course she wasn't looking for someone to be a carbon copy of her late husband—that wouldn't be healthy or reasonable to expect. But she didn't want a tempestuous relationship either; an on-again, off-again showbiz drama really wasn't her idea of a happy life.

Right now, it hurt that Luke could turn on her like that and dump her just because he was in a bad mood. But it would've been far, far worse if she'd actually married Luke and maybe adopted a child with him before something like this happened.

'I'm better off without him,' she told herself briskly.

And if she kept telling herself that, eventually she'd believe it.

'Right. Cut.' George, the director, rolled his eyes. 'Go home, Luke. We're not going to get anything filmed today. You've messed up every single take so far.'

Luke could taste the bitterness in his mouth. His whole life was on the brink of collapse. He couldn't even do his job any more.

And how long would it be before the media picked up on that? How long would it be before directors decided that Luke McKenzie had passed his sell-by date—that Luke McKenzie was no longer a virile male lead but an infertile man, an object of pity?

'Go and get your head sorted out. Talk to your girl,' George advised.

'My girl?' Luke prevaricated. They'd been careful to keep their relationship quiet, on set.

'Everyone knows you're seeing Jess.' George rolled his eyes. 'Just let her talk some sense into you.'

Except Jess wasn't his girl any more, was she? Luke had blown it. Pushed her away. Lashed out at her.

He'd lashed out at Baloo, too. Threatened to send her back to Death Row. And he'd called the press scumbags when his own behaviour had been far, far worse. Shame flooded through him. How could he have been so selfish? How could he have hurt the woman he loved like that?

'Luke?' George asked.

Luke rubbed a hand over his eyes. 'Sorry. I've screwed a lot of things up today, and not just these takes.'

'Yeah, I heard you'd had a fight with

Jess and she'd walked out of the office,' George said.

'I'm an idiot,' Luke told him. 'And I'm not sure she's going to give me the chance to explain myself.'

George looked sympathetic. 'I reckon you're going to need something a hell of a lot better than flowers or chocolates to fix this one.'

'You're telling me,' Luke said wryly. 'I'll see you tomorrow. And I'm sorry, George. I won't screw up tomorrow.'

'Glad to hear it,' George said. 'It would've been helpful if you'd given us some kind of warning about the situation, so the press office could've had contingency plans in place. But the damage is out there, so you might as well go and sort things out with your girl first.'

But before that Luke needed to pick up his dog and apologise to the production manager.

Baloo whined when she saw him, but she stayed by Ayesha's feet, almost cowed.

He sighed. 'I'm sorry, girl. And I apologise for the way I behaved to you, Ayesha.'

'Water off a duck's back. I'm used to stroppy thesps throwing a hissy fit,' Ayesha said. 'But I think there's someone else who deserves a hell of a lot more of an apology.'

'There is,' Luke said. 'And I'm going to be eating humble pie, believe me.'

'If she'll let you.'

'If.' Luke sighed. That was the crunch question. 'Thank you for looking after my dog. And, again, I'm sorry, Ayesha.' He stooped down to make a fuss of Baloo. 'Let's go, sweetie. I'm going to fix this.' Even if he had to sit on Jess's doorstep all day and all night, he'd get her to talk to him. He'd apologise. And hopefully she'd let them start again.

He tried calling her from the car park. There was no answer from her landline or her mobile. Well, that wasn't so surprising. In her shoes, he wouldn't want to talk to him, either. Leaving a message felt too impersonal, so he just put Baloo into her cage so she was safely secured in the back of his car.

What was it Jess had once told him?

When you've had a day of dealing with people you have to be civil to, but really you want to shake them until their teeth rattle and tell them to grow up... That's when a good run with a dog at your side will definitely put the world to rights.

Maybe it would clear his head, too. And he could work out the right words to convince Jess to give him a second chance.

He managed to evade the paparazzi by

using one of the back entrances to the set, and found a park a few miles away where nobody would bother him. Not if he had his beanie hat and glasses on. It would give him just a little while of anonymity. Space to work things out.

He texted Jess before he let Baloo out of the car. *Sorry, I was wrong, please can we talk?*

There was no answer by the time he and Baloo had finished their run. The endorphins had made him feel better, but the guilt was like a heavy sack on his back, weighing him down.

'What am I going to do, Baloo?' he asked.

The dog whined, sat up and put both paws up. Just like in the routine to the song she'd done with Jess.

I love you.

Three simple little words.

OK, Jess was angry with him—and rightfully so—but maybe she'd listen to the dog.

He frowned. It was a long shot. Totally crazy. But if there was the tiniest, tiniest chance, he'd take it.

He downloaded the song he needed and looked at the dog.

'I,' he said, 'am going to teach you something. Something that you've taught me,

Baloo, and I'm sorry it took me so long to work it out.'

The dog looked quizzically at him, her head on one side.

'We're going to dance,' he said.

Not at his place—the paparazzi would have it staked out and he wanted a bit of privacy for this, not someone snooping into his house with a telescopic lens—but he could work with Baloo at Monica's. He called his aunt. 'I need help,' he said. 'I've been an idiot. And I'm being papped so my house is a no-go area right now. Please can I borrow your living room—and maybe ask for a bit of advice?'

To his relief, it turned out that the one other person in his life who meant something to him was still talking to him. Though Monica, too, wasn't impressed with him when he explained what he'd done.

'I know they say you always lash out at the person closest to you—but, Lukey, that was insane.'

'You're telling me,' he said wryly. 'And this is how I'm going to fix it.' He explained his plan to her.

'It's a long shot,' Monica said. 'But I think it's about your only chance, now.'

It took the rest of the afternoon, and it wasn't his best performance ever, but he didn't have time to polish it—and, besides, polish wasn't what Jess needed now. She needed unvarnished honesty.

He drove Baloo over to her flat and rang her doorbell.

No answer.

OK. If she was out, then he'd wait for her. He sat on her front doorstep with Baloo by his side.

Her nosey neighbour came out. 'You do realise dogs aren't allowed?'

'Actually,' Luke said, 'Mr Bright happens to have given this particular dog special dispensation.'

The neighbour stared at him in obvious disbelief.

'What have you got against dogs, anyway?' Luke asked.

'They bite.'

'When they're hurt and scared, maybe,' Luke said. And he was guiltily aware that was what he'd done. He'd bitten Jess metaphorically, like a dog who was scared of being hurt again.

'They're savage beasts,' the neighbour said.

'Most of them aren't, just those who haven't been treated properly or trained. That's what Jess does, trains them.'

'I had to have years of skin grafts,' the neighbour said.

'I'm sorry,' Luke said softly, 'that you had such a bad experience, but not all dogs are bad. Come and meet Baloo. You can't be scared of a dog called Baloo. It's a ridiculous name and she's a ridiculously sweet dog, I promise.'

The neighbour flinched. 'They bite.'

'This one doesn't.' He lifted her up and she licked his face. 'See?'

The neighbour still looked wary.

'Here.' Luke took a dog biscuit from his pocket. 'Put this on your hand and she'll take it from you.'

The neighbour flinched. 'She'll bite me.'

'She won't. I'll stake a thousand pounds on that. A million. Watch.' He put the biscuit in his flattened palm and Baloo took it gently from his hand. 'She won't hurt you,' he reassured the neighbour. Clearly the man had been badly hurt as a child, and nobody had tried to help him overcome his fear of dogs by introducing him to a gentle, kind, ordinary dog.

Maybe Baloo could help him overcome his fear of being hurt again.

The same fear that Luke had to face—except it was emotional rather than physical hurt. And, yes, the dog might just help him, too.

His dog.

'Try it,' Luke said. 'Can we come into your garden?'

'I…' The man shrugged helplessly.

'Thank you,' Luke said, and took Baloo into the garden. 'Sorry, I should've introduced us properly. I'm Luke and this is Baloo.'

'I'm Paul.'

'Nice to meet you, Paul.' Luke shook his hand. 'Baloo, sit and shake hands with Paul.'

The dog dutifully sat and put one paw up.

Paul looked amazed.

'Shake hands,' Luke said softly.

Paul did so—and looked shocked and pleased and amazed, all at the same time.

'Do you want to give her a biscuit to say "well done"?' he asked.

Paul nodded. Luke took another biscuit from his pocket and handed it to Paul.

His hand shaking, Paul gave the dog the biscuit on the flat of his palm.

Baloo was duly gentle and polite as she took it.

'It's OK to stroke her,' Luke said. 'She won't hurt you.'

Paul's hand was unsteady, but he stroked the dog—then flinched as the dog turned her

head and licked him. He stared at the dog, and
then at Luke. 'She licked me.'

'She's a good dog,' Luke said. 'My dog.'

Jess walked into her garden and frowned.
What was her neighbour doing, out in the
front garden? And why was he talking to
Luke? What was Luke doing here?

'What's going on?' she asked.

'I'm introducing my dog to Paul,' Luke
said.

His dog? He was calling Baloo *his* dog?

And...since when had Luke been on first-
name terms with her difficult neighbour?

'While we were waiting for you. Baloo and
I have things to say to you.'

'She's a nice dog,' Paul said, shocking her
further. 'Listen to what they have to say. And
I'm not going to call the landlord.'

'What?' This was totally surreal.

'Will you, Jess? Listen to us?' Luke asked.

'Like you listened to me this morning, you
mean?' She couldn't stop the caustic comment bursting out.

He grimaced. 'I'm an idiot. I got things
very, very wrong. I'm sorry I hurt you, and—'
He broke off and looked at Paul. 'Sorry, do
you mind if this is a private conversation?'

'You're in his garden,' Jess said. 'You can't order the poor man to go indoors.'

'I'm not ordering anyone.' He sighed. 'Jess, please, I need to talk to you—just give me five minutes.'

'Five minutes,' Paul echoed. 'Or I *will* call the landlord—and I'll tell him you have cats as well and they're using the sofa as a scratching post.'

She stared at him. 'You've fallen for the movie star charm as well, have you?'

'Movie star? Who's a movie star? *Him*?' Paul asked, pointing with his thumb at Luke and scoffing. 'He's just a man with a dog.'

'He's right,' Luke agreed. 'I'm just an ordinary man with a dog.'

There was nothing ordinary about Luke, and she was damn sure he knew it. But the Luke McKenzie she'd fallen in love with was nothing like the cold, hard man who'd pushed her away this morning. Which was the real Luke? Could she trust that the Luke she'd fallen for was the real Luke?

'And a gerbil,' Paul added. 'Which has eaten through some of the wiring.'

She put her hands up in the age-old sign of surrender. 'OK. I give in. Five minutes.'

'Shake hands, Baloo,' Paul said, and shook

hands with first Baloo and then with Luke. 'Listen to him, Jess.'

'That was surreal—what did you do to him?' she asked Luke when they were inside her flat.

'You were right about him being lonely—and he was savaged by a dog when he was little. Skin grafts,' Luke said economically.

'Poor man. If I'd realised…'

'Sometimes,' he said, 'we keep our hurt inside and we don't let it out when we should.' He sighed. 'I'm sorry, I've been horrendously unfair to you and I know I don't deserve your time, but please hear us out.'

He fiddled with his phone and then put it on the table. Jess recognised the song from *The Jungle Book* as soon as it started playing, because she'd loved it as a child—'Bare Necessities'. How appropriate for a dog named Baloo.

Baloo was on her hind legs, following Luke, almost like Jess remembered the bear doing in the animated film.

Then she sat down, doing something like the pat-a-cake routine Jess had taught Baloo, for the chorus of the song.

Was this Luke's way of telling her that he loved her?

Could she believe him?

'You're our bare necessity,' he said. 'You're all we want. All we need. And we both love you and want you in our lives.'

'I…I don't know what to say,' she said.

'Baloo's taught me that everyone deserves a second chance. She's my dog, most definitely. I'm giving her that second chance.' He dragged in a breath. 'Will you give me a second chance, Jess?'

'What—so, next time there's a story in the press that upsets you, you can dump me all over again?' she asked.

'No. I was wrong. I guess I've been really angry, this past year. I've damped it all down and told myself that I was over it all—and then today the story was everywhere, and all that anger stopped being buried. It forced its way out, and I took it out on the wrong person. I lashed out at you because…' He wrinkled his nose. 'Well, I guess because I feel close to you.'

She folded her arms and looked at him. No way was she letting him get away with trying to look cute. It wasn't enough.

He grimaced. 'I know just how lame that sounds. I haven't got a script, or flowery words, or anything except what's in my heart, right now, and I hope that's going to be enough.' He blew out a breath. 'I love you,

Jess. You make my world a better place. And I'm so sorry I overreacted this morning and took it out on you.'

'Why did you do it?' she asked.

'Honest truth? Because I'm terrified that they might be right. That I'm not enough of a man.'

She frowned. 'Just because you can't father children, it doesn't mean you're not a man. Fleur was totally wrong about that. Or are you still in love with her?'

'I'm not talking about Fleur. And I'm not in love with her. No way. I love *you*,' he said. 'I'm talking about how Hollywood sees things. What about all the actors and actresses fifty-odd years ago who had to pretend they were straight? If the truth had come out, they would never have worked again. And acting…that's not just what I do, it's who I am. If they don't think I'm enough of a man, then that's the end of me playing the romantic male lead with the slightly posh accent and floppy hair.'

'You honestly think the directors would do that?'

'It's not necessarily the directors. It's the marketing people. The people with the money.' He shrugged. 'I don't have any control over that.'

'Your fans would be pretty upset if you didn't work again,' she said. 'And does it have to be Hollywood? Why can't you make your own low-budget film here in England? Direct it yourself?'

'That,' he said, 'never occurred to me.' He looked thoughtful. 'An indie film. If the script was right. Direct. Yes, I could.'

'So the worst doesn't *have* to be the worst.'

'No,' he admitted.

'You've built up this huge fear of losing your career—like my neighbour being scared of dogs. You just need someone to show you that things aren't as bad as you think they are,' she said.

'Maybe not in career terms, but the rest of my life's pretty much a train wreck at the moment. I finally find someone I can be myself with—someone who makes me smile for all the right reasons, someone who makes me want to be a better man. And then I'm stupid enough to let her go. Can you forgive me, Jess? Can we wipe the slate clean and start again?'

'You really want to be with me?'

'I really want to be with you,' he said. 'But sometimes I can be a real idiot. I can't necessarily offer you an easy time. I can't give you children. I have to go where my work is, and the location isn't always in England. And, any time we have a fight, there's a good chance it'll be splashed right across the press, because that's the kind of garbage they thrive on.'

She looked thoughtful. 'OK. Those are the cons. And the pros?'

He frowned. 'Pros?'

'If you're doing a risk assessment, there are always good points as well as bad,' she said.

She was going to listen to him. Maybe give him that second chance, if he was honest with her and kept nothing else back.

Luke's heart felt as if it had swollen to twice its normal size. He knew it was anatomically impossible, but he could still feel the hope blooming out, filling him.

'Good points. OK. I've got a nice view from my living room and great walks on my doorstep. I live with the best dog in the world—a dog who can dance with you if you're feeling down, and who seems to be developing a bit of a bossy streak and tells you what to do.' He smiled at her. 'And I love you. I hope that counts for something.'

'It counts,' she said. 'OK. The pros all work for me. Back to the cons.'

Where it could all go wrong. But he knew that they needed to sort this out.

'You're an idiot—agreed, and we can work on that. Life isn't easy—well, that's true whether you're a movie star or not. Children…' She spread her hands. 'Yes. I do want children. But this is the twenty-first century. We have options. We can foster, we can adopt, we can try IVF—if it's what we both want, we'll find a way to make it work.' She frowned. 'You don't work all the time in England. OK. Sometimes I can be with you on location, sometimes I'll be here with Baloo, and there's always the phone and Skype when we're apart. The world's a much smaller place now, so you working away isn't that big a deal. And the press…' She sighed. 'I guess we'll just have to put up with that. As long as we know the truth and the people who matter to us know the truth, and we talk about things instead of jumping to conclusions or going off in a strop, that's enough.'

Thank God.

She was going to let him be enough for her.

He dropped to one knee. 'Jess Greenacre, despite the fact that I'm an idiot, I'm prepared to work on it. I love you. Will you marry me and spend your life with me—me and you and a dog named Baloo?' He smacked a palm to his forehead. 'I'm supposed to have a ring when I do this. I told you I was an idiot.'

'Not an idiot. Maybe just a little under-rehearsed.' But she was laughing as she dropped to her knees to meet him. 'Luke McKenzie— I love you, too, and yes, I'll marry you.'

And Baloo put her paws up as if to echo both of them.

I love you.

* * * * *

COMING NEXT MONTH FROM

HARLEQUIN®

Romance

Available May 6, 2014

#4423 EXPECTING THE PRINCE'S BABY
by Rebecca Winters

When widower prince Vicenzo's wife of convenience dies after their royal surrogate becomes pregnant, he's faced with a dilemma: respect royal protocol? Or follow his heart...and wed the mother of his child!

#4424 THE MILLIONAIRE'S HOMECOMING
by Cara Colter

When widow Kayla literally falls in the path of childhood friend David, she knows it can't be just fate. Are they being given a chance to rewrite history—*together...*?

#4425 THE HEIR OF THE CASTLE
by Scarlet Wilson

Left to arrange the inheritance of Annick Castle, Callan is captivated by potential heir Laurie. Callan cannot afford a distraction—but nor can he afford to ignore his heart!

#4426 SWEPT AWAY BY THE TYCOON
by Barbara Wallace

Chloe is used to flying solo—until former soldier Ian Black sweeps her off her feet! Dare she believe the most heartwarming truth of all—that the best men stick around forever?

YOU CAN FIND MORE INFORMATION ON UPCOMING HARLEQUIN® TITLES, FREE EXCERPTS AND MORE AT WWW.HARLEQUIN.COM.

LARGER-PRINT BOOKS!
GET 2 FREE LARGER-PRINT NOVELS PLUS
2 FREE GIFTS!

✦ HARLEQUIN®

Romance

From the Heart, For the Heart

YES! Please send me 2 FREE LARGER-PRINT Harlequin® Romance novels and my 2 FREE gifts (gifts are worth about $10). After receiving them, if I don't wish to receive any more books, I can return the shipping statement marked "cancel." If I don't cancel, I will receive 4 brand-new novels every month and be billed just $4.84 per book in the U.S. or $5.24 per book in Canada. That's a savings of at least 19% off the cover price! It's quite a bargain! Shipping and handling is just 50¢ per book in the U.S. and 75¢ per book in Canada.* I understand that accepting the 2 free books and gifts places me under no obligation to buy anything. I can always return a shipment and cancel at any time. Even if I never buy another book, the two free books and gifts are mine to keep forever.

119/319 HDN F43Y

Name	(PLEASE PRINT)

Address	Apt. #

City	State/Prov.	Zip/Postal Code

Signature (if under 18, a parent or guardian must sign)

Mail to the **Harlequin® Reader Service:**
IN U.S.A.: P.O. Box 1867, Buffalo, NY 14240-1867
IN CANADA: P.O. Box 609, Fort Erie, Ontario L2A 5X3
Want to try two free books from another line?
Call 1-800-873-8635 or visit www.ReaderService.com.

* Terms and prices subject to change without notice. Prices do not include applicable taxes. Sales tax applicable in N.Y. Canadian residents will be charged applicable taxes. Offer not valid in Quebec. This offer is limited to one order per household. Not valid for current subscribers to Harlequin Romance Larger-Print books. All orders subject to credit approval. Credit or debit balances in a customer's account(s) may be offset by any other outstanding balance owed by or to the customer. Please allow 4 to 6 weeks for delivery. Offer available while quantities last.

Your Privacy—The Harlequin® Reader Service is committed to protecting your privacy. Our Privacy Policy is available online at www.ReaderService.com or upon request from the Harlequin Reader Service.

We make a portion of our mailing list available to reputable third parties that offer products we believe may interest you. If you prefer that we not exchange your name with third parties, or if you wish to clarify or modify your communication preferences, please visit us at www.ReaderService.com/consumerchoice or write to us at Harlequin Reader Service Preference Service, P.O. Box 9062, Buffalo, NY 14269. Include your complete name and address.

"NOW, SEVEN WEEKS LATER, here Abby was with the prince
of every woman's dreams riding to the top of the mountain.
But there was nothing normal about his life or hers. When
she and her father had gone through all the what-ifs before
she'd made her decision to be a surrogate, the idea of either
Michelina or Vincenzo dying had only been mentioned in
passing. But she couldn't have imagined anything so horrible
and never thought about it again.

"Shall we go in?" said the deep, velvety male voice next
to her.

"Oh—yes!" Abby had been so immersed in thought she
hadn't realized they'd arrived. Night had fallen during their
journey here. Vincenzo led her off the funicular and walked
her through a hallway to another set of doors. They opened
onto a terrace with a candlelit table and flowers set for two.

A small gasp of pleasure escaped her lips to realize she
was looking out over the same view she could see from her
own patio at the palace. But they were much higher up, so
she could take in the whole city of Arancia alive with lights
for the nightly festival celebration.

"What an incredible vista."

"I agree," he murmured as he helped her to sit. Of course

it was an accident that his hand brushed her shoulder, but she felt his touch like she'd just come into contact with an electric current. This was so wrong, she was terrified.

"Mind if I ask you a personal question?" Vincenzo asked.

How personal? She was on dangerous ground, fearing he could see right through her, to her chaotic innermost thoughts. "What would you like to know?"

"Has there been an important man in your life? And if so, why didn't you marry him?"

Yes. I'm looking at him.

Heat filled her cheeks. "I had my share of boyfriends, but by college I got serious about my studies. Law school doesn't leave time for much of a social life when you're clerking for a judge who expects you to put in one hundred and twenty hours a week."

"Sounds like one of my normal days," he remarked. She knew he wasn't kidding. "You and I never discussed this before, but I'm curious about something. Didn't you ever want to be a mother to your own child first?"

Abby stifled her moan. If he only knew how during her teenage years she'd dreamed about being married to him and having his baby. Since that time, history had been made and she was carrying his baby in real life. *But it wasn't hers, and that dream had come with a price.* How could she be feeling like this when he was forbidden to her?

EXPECTING THE PRINCE'S BABY
by Rebecca Winters is available May 2014 only from Harlequin® Romance—don't miss it!